AMELIA ANNE IS DEAD AND GONE

— Kat Rosenfield —

AMELIA ANNE IS DEAD AND GONE

DUTTON BOOKS
a member of Penguin Group (USA) Inc.

Published by the Penguin Group
Penguin Group (USA) Inc., 375 Hudson Street, New York, New York 10014, U.S.A.
Penguin Group (Canada), 90 Eglinton Avenue East, Suite 700, Toronto, Ontario, Canada M4P 2Y3
(a division of Pearson Penguin Canada Inc.)
Penguin Books Ltd, 80 Strand, London WC2R 0RL, England
Penguin Ireland, 25 St Stephen's Green, Dublin 2, Ireland (a division of Penguin Books Ltd)
Penguin Group (Australia), 250 Camberwell Road, Camberwell, Victoria 3124, Australia
(a division of Pearson Australia Group Pty Ltd)
Penguin Books India Pvt Ltd, 11 Community Centre, Panchsheel Park, New Delhi—110 017, India
Penguin Group (NZ), 67 Apollo Drive, Rosedale, Auckland 0632, New Zealand
(a division of Pearson New Zealand Ltd.)
Penguin Books (South Africa) (Pty) Ltd, 24 Sturdee Avenue, Rosebank, Johannesburg 2196, South Africa
Penguin Books Ltd, Registered Offices: 80 Strand, London WC2R 0RL, England

CIP Data is available.

Published in the United States by Dutton Books,
a member of Penguin Group (USA) Inc.
345 Hudson Street, New York, New York 10014
www.penguin.com/teen

Designed by Elynn Cohen
Printed in USA
First Edition

10 9 8 7 6 5 4 3 2 1

ISBN 978-0-525-42389-8

for Brad.
I owe you a solid.

AMELIA ANNE IS DEAD AND GONE

PROLOGUE

The night before Amelia Anne Richardson bled her life away on a parched dirt road outside of town, I bled out my dignity in the back of a pickup truck under a star-pricked sky.

The back of a pickup truck. A country song, jukebox cliché. I was eighteen.

Afterward, the late-night mosquitoes floated out of the dark to settle on my thighs. Hovering and sucking at my skin, drawn in by the thick, mingling scents of sex and sweat and summer.

I swatted them away and lay back alone on the oil-stained steel, legs twisted into the scratchy cheap fabric of a K-Mart sleeping bag, propped dizzily on my elbows, examining the moisture collecting under me by the weak glow of the moon and the dashboard lights. James was a silhouette in the cab, nonchalantly smoking and tapping his knuckles against the window glass. His sweat dried on my skin. The sound of blood in my ears, rushing and receding with each breath, pulsed in time with the flare at the end of his cigarette. He inhaled, the cherry glowing, illuminating his mouth. His teeth were slick pearls behind the filter.

That afternoon, I'd walked across a rickety platform to collect my high school diploma from the principal—a beaming man with sweat-darkened patches on his collared shirt, a man whose mouth stretched with broad, smiling pride when the highest achievers of the graduating class laid one hand on the rolled slip of paper and the other in his outstretched palm. Hearty handshakes all around for the top kids: the bright future–havers, the scholarship winners, the team captains, the college bound.

He nodded at me, the salutatorian, the aspiring lawyer, bound for a high-powered life in a city far away. "I know you'll go far," he said as he pumped my hand.

But then, after the photos were taken and cheeks kissed and polyester gowns shucked off like a snake's skin, I'd gone only as far as the outskirts of town, where James turned the truck down a rutted road through the woods, into an open field, and parked with a jolt on the rough grass.

Parked under a wide-open sky pricked by thousands of stars.

Parked his hand between my legs and half threw me out the tiny back window and into the flatbed, where my feet flew over my head and I scrabbled for purchase on slippery steel. I peered back at him; he smiled, shrugged.

"Ha," he said.

"You can't throw the salutatorian around like that," I said.

A sleeping bag came through the window next, and then James himself, all long legs and arms. He was long, lanky, the most spiderlike boy I had ever seen. His Adam's apple bobbed on his fleshless neck. Skinny wrists gave way to huge, bony hands with knuckles that gnarled and knobbed like an old man's. He exited the cab, his clothes whispering against the glass. I lay down.

Graduation night, too-smooth boyfriend with a beater pickup and no diploma of his own, the sky full of stars and the night full of chirping crickets—a perfect, planned-out, teenaged tableau. This wasn't the first time I'd been here, not even the first time I'd thought that I was too tired, the truck bed too dirty, but gone ahead anyway, letting him groan and shudder on top of me until he'd finished and lay his damp, musty hair against my chest. I liked the sex, sometimes. But more than that, I liked the closeness of afterward, the way his skinny arms would wrap around me and we'd lie, tangled and warm, breathing moist air into each other's mouth. And this day, they'd told us, was ours. A step into the future. And now, right now, a moment for two bright young things on the verge of the rest of their lives to stop, strip, and spend one more night—one more hot, beautiful, stagnant summer—together in the back of a pickup.

James straddled my hips, grappling with the glinting button on my jeans, baring my legs and belly to the breathless openness of the blue-black sky. His shoulder pressed into my open mouth, and I could taste the damp cloth of his T-shirt against my tongue.

It was quick.

He didn't say a word, didn't make a sound, and neither did I. Not until, with his sweat still drying on my skin and his scent still draped over my body, he pulled back and looked down at me. In the dark, his features were nothing but vague lights and shadows.

His voice came from somewhere above me.

"This is the last time we'll ever do this."

I laughed at first.

"We've got all summer," I started to say. All summer to be here, be together. The words died on my lips as he looked back at me.

"We're done," he said. "This is done."

I inhaled, one deep breath. Our eyes met. His were opaque. Mine were swimming. When he moved away, I only knew by the sudden sensation of air—cool and empty, moving over my thighs.

It was over in minutes, seconds, in the flutter of an eyelid. I gaped up at the place where his face had been moments before, blinking, seeing only the stars partially obliterated by a thick piece of hair that had fallen over my face. I thought about crying—thought about screaming, begging—but my throat had seamed itself shut. My jeans were twisted into an impossible knot around my knee.

I disentangled myself from the twisted sleeping bag. Kicked the crumple of denim off my leg, thinking to myself, *it's a little late for dignity.* I laid back on my elbows and watched James. Watched him wrap his sensual mouth around one cigarette after another. Watched the sweat and slick evaporate from my thighs.

Later, I would sink down into a bathtub full of scalding hot water, lay my swollen eyelids against the cool porcelain, and shake so hard that my bones made soft clinking sounds against the tub. Later, I would toss back four painkillers against my clenching throat, and let my thoughts ramble and circle back again to James's heavy-lidded eyes and hard, clutching hands. To an article I'd once read that included the phrase, "For many, the emotional trauma of a broken heart can manifest as real, physical pain"—and that I thought, at the time, was the stupidest thing I had ever heard.

In the corner, above the sink, the small black second hand of the clock silently ticked away toward midnight.

It was still graduation day.

CHAPTER 1

*T*hey found her just after dawn on June 24th, crumpled awkwardly by the side of the road with a rust-colored blossom drying in the dirt beneath her.

Grant Willard, a rough man who worked the overnight shift at the stationer's plant outside of town, was the one who saw her first. Later, he told anyone who would listen that he'd thought someone had left a bag of clothes lying in the dirt there, where the snaking curves of County Road 128 crossed briefly over Route 9 and then veered off toward the swelling, distant Appalachians.

"Looked like a damn rag doll," he announced to an enthralled crowd at the local bar later that night. He tugged on the scraggly beard that grew in burnt-orange patches on his chin. Drops of Bud Light accumulated in his mustache.

"Just all jumbled up together like that, looked like someone threw her out of a truck and kept right on going."

"Was she naked?" another man asked. He pronounced it *nekkid*. The bartender, a woman with a home perm and a mouth that bled lipstick in cracked, radiating lines, rolled her eyes and snorted.

"No, man," Grant said. "She had on some kind of dress thing. She looked all crumpled up, kinda boneless, like, in a pile." He paused. "Yeah, like a boneless pile."

He liked the sound of that and said it a few more times, smacking the top of the bar for emphasis, before one of the ladies on a neighboring stool turned to him and said, "Grant, shut the fuck up."

Grant, a local celebrity for a few weeks after the incident, didn't mention that he'd been near to falling asleep at the wheel, drifting toward the shoulder when he recognized a human form in the dust at the side of the road. He had jerked the wheel hard to the left and then skidded to a stop just past the body, with his truck straddling the faded yellow centerline, gaping in the rearview mirror at what was definitely a woman's delicate arm outstretched toward the pavement. He told no one the full truth. He had seen her, sure, but seen her too late. He had run over her fingers. Breakable bones, the tiny phalanges and brittle carpals, splayed and splintered in the gravel. Ivory dust mixed with rough rock, but no blood. She was dry, dry inside like a ten-thousand-year-old tomb, with the last of her life barely dampening the dirt underneath.

Within twenty-four hours, there wasn't a person in town who didn't know the story: how the dead girl lay in the dirt, how the state police blocked the road and avoided looking at her while they worked, how the day turned so swiftly, blistering hot. Choking waves shimmered, rose in stifling S curves from the pavement while the men mopped their foreheads and guzzled water and professed exasperated bafflement over the dead body that lay at their feet. Before they came, just after dawn, the hometown cops—both just twenty years old, both local boys—stood awkwardly over her as they waited for someone with more experience to show up. They shuffled in the dirt, admonished each other by turns not to disturb anything, stole sidelong glances at the body.

"What the hell was she doing out here, anyway?" said Stan Murray, who was still trying to regain his credibility after leaping away from the corpse fifteen minutes earlier when a passing truck caused tiny vibrations in her dead fingers.

"*Aaaagh!*" he had screamed in a stunning soprano voice. "*It's moving!*"

Jack Francis, his blue polyester policeman's shirt unbuttoned as far as decency would allow, exposing the kinky, straw-colored hair that spilled over his undershirt collar, rubbed a dust-darkened finger against his chin.

"She bled out right here," he said authoritatively, hands in pockets and indicating the rust-colored stain on the ground with one pointed toe. "Someone probably brought her out here just to do this. Premeditated, and all."

"Who is she?" asked Stan, reaching toward the ragged

skirt bunched around spindly, ashen legs, studiously ignoring the stains in his single-minded quest for identification. Jack swatted his hand away.

"That's a skirt, Murray. She doesn't have any fucking pockets. Get your fingers away from the evidence."

Stan squatted dangerously close, more blue polyester straining against his ample backside, holster sticking awkwardly off his hip.

"Jack, you ever seen anything like this?"

"Dead body, you mean?"

"No, everyone's seen a dead body, man, I mean like this." Stan's gesturing hand passed over the woman—the life wrung out in bruises beneath her eyes, soaking and blooming and drying in the dirt, as he waved his palm over her breasts and the curve of her hip and her delicate, motionless face. Rice-paper skin slack over hard, hard bone. Even like this, you could see that she'd been pretty.

Jack turned away and stared up the road, away from the strange intimacy of Stan's hand making its slow journey through the air above the dead woman, up at the heat-distorted shape that would soon reveal itself to be a caravan of police cruisers.

"Never seen a dead body at all, to be honest," he muttered, gritting his teeth against the swirling dust and squinting at the line of cars, slowly coming into focus.

Jittery chatter gave way to machismo posturing as the police chief's cruiser pulled up. Beside it, crime scene workers disembarked from a van and made cautious circles in the dust, searching. One of them held up a cigarette butt. Jack Francis visibly stiffened next to him. He turned toward the younger man. "Officer, something wrong?"

"Sorry . . . that's mine."

The chief of police, a man with a deeply creased face and shiny, bald pate, who for twenty years had been fighting the urge to call younger officers "son," beckoned Jack toward him.

"Son," he said, "it'd be a good thing if you tried *not* to single-handedly mess up the entire crime scene."

Jack reddened. "No, sir."

Stan Murray, emboldened by the presence of the other men, sidled over to the place where Officer Jack Francis stood, red-faced and with hands still jammed into his pockets.

"That was smooth."

Jack didn't answer. Stan's smile faded into a look of discomfort.

"Fuck you," said Jack, finally, but without venom. The two stood together, looking lost, too young to buy booze or grow a beard. They shifted from left foot to right, hands finding purchase in pockets, groping for cigarettes, chain smoking and straddling the faded yellow line that was criss-crossed by the snaking skid marks of Grant Willard's unfortunate truck. They turned together to watch the by-the-book movements of the state police as they circled, measured, photographed, lifted cold limbs and then let them fall. They stared toward the specter of death that lay in a heap on the side of the road.

Innocence can only last so long, especially that kind that comes from growing up sheltered by quiet neighborhoods, immaculate concrete sidewalks, so much nothingness for miles around. Kids riding plastic Big Wheel bikes too fast down dead-end streets; spills taken on sharp corners; asphalt picked out of knees and elbows that bleed, scab over, then heal. Same faces, same streets, day in and day out, eyes that never witness anything more desolate than those empty, gravel-strewn county roads. And then, one day and all at once, the veil lifts. Jack and Stan, looking miserably at their feet and each other, knew this.

The dead girl, whose name no one knew yet, lay still. Her wide-open eyes, glazed, dead eyes, fixed their milky gaze on the Appalachians, looked up to the last patch of asphalt where County Road 128 turned a corner and vanished. The mountains swallowed it. The men looked at her as she looked away from them. Seeing Amelia, who saw nothing at all.

CHAPTER 2

The phone in our house rang seven times between the hours of ten and eleven o'clock that morning. The calls began as soon as Grant's story had made its way around town, starting with the gas station attendant at the corner of Main Street and Route 7, passing lightning-fast over country roads and quiet streets, tumbling from one mouth to another so quickly that, for fifteen minutes, every phone in the village of Bridgeton rang busy. People buzzed and hummed and speculated. It seemed impossible that the dead girl, the rag doll on the road-shoulder, could remain anonymous for long. Not with everybody talking about her, her, her.

The first six calls were spreading the news. It flooded in from neighbors, fellow gardeners, supermarket shoppers whose elbows would brush against my mother's when they stood side by side and reached for the shrink-wrapped, violet-veined chicken cutlets in our grocery's meat section. Ladies who frosted their hair and cropped it short in sensible, stylish bobs. They sipped lemonade in their shabby chic kitchens, pressed fingers to the dial pad, spilled the sensationalism of our mysterious tragedy into the receiver. Jaws wagged all over town.

My mother sat, listening—interested at first, then simply patient. She hung up with a sigh, turned toward me with a hand in her thick hair.

"A girl was killed last night," she told me. "Just outside of town."

The words were out of place in our relentlessly cheerful kitchen. Rays of sunlight originated somewhere within the neatly poured glasses of orange juice and flooded over, drenched the tablecloth, poured onto the sweet, printed wallpaper and around the shelves decorated with retro-red mixing bowls and vintage-inspired placards that read MAKE IT WITH JELL-O!, gently draped the gingham tablecloth and white-painted wood chairs.

I was smothering a biscuit with jelly, drowning it in purple before taking a bite. My stomach clenched, painfully, my throat constricted, I choked and then forced it down, putting the uneaten remainder back on my plate where it would remain untouched. The previous night's events were in my mouth—there it was, my little story, bitter and bad tasting. It was unpalatable, too sour to swallow and too ugly to spit out.

He fucked me, and then he left me.

I couldn't say it—not here, with the juice and sunshine and china.

"What?" I said.

"A girl," she said, again. "Or young woman—they found her body early this morning. That was Lena on the phone, she heard it from. . . . well, who knows, but the police are out there now. They don't know who she is."

"Where?"

"Out by One Twenty-eight, where it crosses Nine. But I wouldn't go out there right now, even if there was something to see I wouldn't want you to—"

"No, Mom, no, that's not what I meant. Morbid curiosity. I don't want to see." I put a hand to my temple, pushed my plate away. The tablecloth bunched and rose in folds underneath it. The orange juice glowed brighter. It was radioactive. It was hurting my eyes.

"Are you sick, honey?" my mom asked. She put a hand on the crown of my head, put her upper lip to my forehead, checking for a temperature. The gesture was achingly familiar. For as long as I could remember, my mother's soft upper lip had been the litmus test for ailments of all kinds. It foretold the future, discerned cold from flu, measured fever within a tenth of a degree. I wanted to cry.

"I think I'm okay," I said.

"You got in pretty late last night," she said. "Aren't you tired? Maybe you'd like to take a nap on the sunporch."

"Okay," I said, and all at once, I did. I would lie on the creaky white wicker sofa, wrapped up in a blanket that was soft knit and covered in yarn pills, feeling the tickle of stray hairs on my forehead as a backyard breeze swished by. I thought about the dappled light that bathed the afternoon, and the rustling, *shhh, shhh* sound of the trees. I thought of the drowning moment when sleep overtook, when sight, sound, and touch vanished behind closed eyes, and of how good it would feel to leave behind last night and its gritty, pained aftermath. Just for now. Just for a little while.

I thought, too, of the dead girl, somewhere at the base of the Appalachians, waiting anonymously in the dirty heat for someone to make sense of whatever was left of her.

My eyes closed over the summer afternoon. I sighed toward unconsciousness.

My last thought, slipping by like one of the brief shadows cast by the rustling trees, was that my field—the one where, twelve hours before, I had sat in silent shock while the boy I loved tore our carefully made plans to shreds—was only steps down the road from where the body lay.

Shhh, the trees said.

I hushed.

Drifted.

Slept.

Until call number seven, his voice on the line.

It was James who'd heard the story first, James who came up on Grant Willard's Ford, waiting to pull away from the police barracks on Institution Road. He had slowed, chin-bobbed at the other driver to *Go ahead, man*, before he spotted Grant. Not in his grit-streaked truck, but on the side of the road, emptying his guts into an appalled patch of black-eyed Susans.

Grant turned, wiping beer bile from his whiskers.

"Rough night, Grant?"

"Shit, man, I just came from the cops. There's a dead body out on One Twenty-eight. Damn near ran her over."

Even in the mess he'd made, James still turned to me first when he had something to say. The ringing phone cut through the soft wash of sleep, and then my mother was shaking my foot and saying, "Honey, honey?"

"Yeah," I said sleepily, lifting my head.

"It's James on the phone."

Something must have registered on my face, because she pressed her hand to the receiver and mouthed, *Should I say you're not here?* I shook my head, reached for the phone. She handed it to me, gave my foot another reassuring pat, and retreated back into the kitchen. I had started to sweat inside the blanket. I kicked it off.

"Hello," I said, holding the phone to my mouth. My words felt hollow, guarded.

"Hey."

"Hey."

There was silence for a minute, the two of us measuring each other to the sound of breath echoing in the receiver. Me, willing myself not to cry and wondering whether I'd somehow imagined the whole thing. Wondering whether he'd even meant to call. I could picture him—finger on the keypad, dialing on groggy autopilot, remembering too late that things had changed.

I wasn't his girl anymore.

James finally spoke again.

"So, there's a dead girl in the road up by One Twenty-eight."

"I heard."

"From who?"

"Mom's friends have been calling all morning."

"Gossiping old biddies," he said.

"Of which you are one," I said automatically, and when James laughed I surprised myself by joining in with a weak chuckle. My laughter was brittle, but it was a shared moment, and the aftermath hit me with painful force. This shouldn't be happening.

Our shared moments were over.

We're done.

I wanted to scream into the receiver, but knew that if I opened my mouth, all that would come out was raw, sobbing hurt. The trees were sighing. Leaves flipped over in the wind, exposing their pallid, veined undersides. The breeze rushed in the receiver and mixed with my own shallow breath.

"Where are you?" James asked.

"On the porch."

"I can hear the wind."

I swallowed and prayed that my voice would stay even. "James?"

The line was silent, but I could feel him. Waiting.

"James," I said, again.

"Yes."

"I don't understand why you're calling me."

"Rebecca, I—"

He stopped. I waited. I could hear him now, grinding his teeth. I knew the sound. He did it when he wanted to say something but couldn't put it together properly.

I waited.

In the seconds that passed, I began to wonder if I'd lost my mind. If it hadn't happened—or at least, hadn't happened the way I remembered. In the bright light of day it seemed too brutal to be real, my recollection too inexact. The opaque blanket of that blue-black dark obscured it the way it had blurred James's features as he looked down on me. I struggled, but couldn't make the memory brighter than the faint glow of the dashboard and the burning flare at the end of his cigarette.

Only my swollen eyelids and churning gut told me that something had happened last night.

"I don't know what to say to you," I said. "Last night—I mean, you . . ."

"I want to see you," he said.

"Why do you want to see me?" I bit the words off as my voice cracked, felt the last tenuous threads of self-control slipping away. "Why would I want to see you?"

"I don't know. I guess, last night . . ." he trailed off. "You're angry at me?"

I sat in silence, fighting the urge to snap back. *No shit*, I wanted to say.

"Rebecca?"

Had I imagined it?

He cleared his throat. "Please . . . don't be mad."

Impossible.

"James," I said. My voice was a dead thing, flat and toneless. "Did you or did you not break up with me last night?"

At first, he didn't answer. I heard the *skritch* of flint, the short sucking inhale as he lit a cigarette.

"I don't know."

I don't know.

I tried to make that fit—to reimagine last night as something less final, something other than an execution, something nebulous and misunderstandable that left us neither together nor apart. Not done, not undone.

It seemed impossible that something which had felt so brutal and decisive to me could feel to him like limbo.

But I wanted to believe him. I had trusted James, and in return, he had loved me, protected me, kept my secrets. In his eyes, even more than in mine, we were always solid.

"Rebecca, let's talk. I want to see you."

"Don't do me any favors," I said bitterly. "If this is just going to be a rerun of last night—"

"That's not what I meant."

"What is it you want to say?" I pushed.

"Will you listen?"

"I don't know. Is what you're going to say worth listening to?"

"I don't know," he said, urgency creeping into his voice. "But I'm coming."

CHAPTER 3

*I*t had started the year before, in August, with only two short weeks left before the weather turned cool and the town's youth returned, plodding and en masse, to school. Our first meeting was romantic. High school legend-like, it made me yearn to stay with him just for the chance to tell our someday-kids about how their father had swept me off my feet at the tender age of sixteen. About the bonfire at Hunter's Point and the coltish-skinny, cigarette-smoking boy with shaggy hair, sitting apart from his friends, who looked across the flames at me with such intensity that he himself seemed to be on fire. Saturday nights since God knows when had been spent this way: Bridgeton's kids piled into beater cars with beer-laden backseats and drove like a steel caravan out to the lake's lonely northern point. It was a homogenous group—nobody under sixteen, nobody over twenty, nobody who didn't still call our quiet town home. The unspoken rule: When you moved on, when you moved away, you didn't come here anymore.

And if, when your twenty-first birthday came around, you were still here, then they were waiting for you at the East Bank Tavern—ready to offer you a seat at the bar that would be yours for as long as it took, for as long as you needed it. Forever, if that's what you wanted.

James and I had stared at each other for what seemed like hours, cheeks glowing with the heat, while other people flitted in and out on the periphery, like light-drawn moths, sucking on the necks of bottles that held watery beer. He was wearing jeans with the knees ripped out, threadbare and fringed where the fabric had torn. I stared at the loose threads, white-hot in the firelight. I was sure they would incinerate, and sure that my eyelashes were smoldering, melting, painting black track marks of soot against my skin. I stared back at him, feeling my skin grow tighter against the onslaught of heat. It took too much time, took ages, for him to come around to where I knelt in the dirt, my beer untouched beside me and sand clinging to my knees.

"Come for a walk with me," he'd said.

"What, you mean *alone?*" I'd replied, teasing, my cheeks flushing with relief as I turned away from the fire. His face had stayed the same, impenetrable, neutral and firm.

I would see that expression, or lack thereof, over and over in the future, every time I made light of things he found serious. He was fixated, intent, and beyond amusement.

"Come with me," he'd repeated.

And I, body humming like a live wire, not a bit afraid, had gone.

We had walked through the tangled vines, tall creek-side trees, weaving through the swamp with its wet holes that sucked at our ankles and threatened to steal our shoes at the slightest misstep. We didn't speak. The fire behind us, the light growing fainter, punctuated the night with pops and crackles as the wood burned, releasing showers of sparks into the air. We could hear them behind us, the other kids, shrieking with glee as smoke rose into the night.

James took a long drag on his cigarette, his cheeks sinking inward, pulling the smoke deep into his chest. He turned toward me, looked at me through the curtain of hair that fell over his dark eyes. For the first time since we'd left the fire, I felt unsure of myself.

I cocked a hand on my hip with fake nonchalance.

"Are you going to offer me a cigarette, or what?" I said.

"What?"

"I said—"

"Come on, you don't smoke," he said, waving his hand at me and settling on the horizontal trunk of a fallen tree. It was enormous, cushioned with deep, pungent moss.

"How do you know?" I said, positioning myself with one leg tucked under me, turned toward him. "You don't know me; I could be at two packs a day. Running for the cancer train at a hundred miles an hour."

"The cancer train, I like that."

"Do you?"

"It's got a ring to it. But it doesn't matter. You still don't smoke." He looked at me, his lips curling in the beginning of a smile.

"Maybe not. But," I said, leaning toward him, "I'm feeling reckless."

The tree creaked underneath us. He shook his head and then slid a cigarette out of the pack, lit it with the burning tip of his own, presented it to me with a flourish. I took it and inhaled, praying that I wouldn't embarrass myself by coughing. He was right, of course—I didn't smoke. I exhaled, blowing the thin stream upward, toward the overhead crochet of treetops.

"So, it's James?" I said.

"Right," he said.

"James, like James Dean."

"Right again."

"What are you, a rebel? High school dropout, smoker for life?"

He eyed me.

"Who says I'm a high school dropout."

"You're not?"

He shook his head.

"I thought you quit last year," I said. "We had a history class together, didn't we? I saw you there three times, tops, then you stopped coming."

"I'd already fucked it up by October," he said. "They wanted me to repeat. 'Failure due to absences.' I didn't see the point in staying when it'd be the same exact thing next year. Memorizing it all, all over again, dates and names and whatever . . . I couldn't."

"Makes sense, I guess. You didn't need to leave in a huff, though."

"They didn't need to fail me," he said, looking straight ahead. "They could have understood, figured something out."

"Why would they?"

"My mom was sick. She was . . ." He paused and swallowed, hard. "She was dying. She died."

I started to touch him, then thought better of it.

"And they still failed you?"

"Yeah."

"Did you tell them your mom was sick?"

"They knew."

"They knew?" I said. "They just knew; you didn't tell them?"

"It's a small town. They knew, all right," he said, jamming the half-smoked cigarette savagely against the tree trunk. He moved an inch, about to stand, then changed his mind. He pulled another cigarette from the pack and lit it.

"Okay, so they knew," I prompted.

He looked right at me, squared off, jaw set.

"I don't want to talk about this right now," he said. "Let's just say that things have been hard this year."

Things were hard for James. Harder for him than for anyone else I'd known, before or since. He did it to himself, in a way—refusing anyone's help, nearly incapacitated at times by his anger at the hand fate had dealt him.

He was a victim of circumstance. His family, what was left of it, still lived in a whitewashed, falling-down house out in the woods, which stood as though unsure of itself in between two big pines. It was a skeleton of a house, bleached bone outside, rickety railings wrapping a splintering porch, a crumbling foundation under years of dead leaves. His mom dead, his dad turned cold and quiet by grief; the money gone into hospital bills and hours of treatments and endless vials of pills to take the edge off of her pain.

His room was high up, under the eaves. I went there only once, where I walked through haunted hallways and climbed the stairs to the third floor while he vanished into another part of the house. One visit was enough. I'd trailed my fingers over the undusted banister, the surfaces of photographs. I had lain down across his bed—still flannel-covered in the late spring, no sensible mother there to make the seasonal switch—and imagined him grasping for sleep there while a dying woman's screams echoed up the stairwell and sank into the walls. Cancer had eaten her alive.

I pictured him in bed, face turned to the window with dawn breaking outside, succumbing to exhaustion and drifting for hours, while his alarm rang on and on and on. Waking up at noon, another day of school missed, another morning wasted. His mother in the kitchen, James beside her. The two of them, together, his grief, her clawlike hands. She would stroke his hair. He would cry.

I had still been lying there, breathing in deep to catch the musky scent of James's hair that clung to the hunters' plaid pillow, nearly asleep, when he came upstairs to find me. I heard him come in. I didn't open my eyes. I listened to him grinding his teeth in the doorway. I wanted to rise up, away from my body, to sit on the beams overhead and look down to watch him watching me. I wanted him to move forward, touch my cheek, wake me from the sleep that I was faking and tell me it was time to go.

Eventually, I opened my eyes. He hadn't moved from the doorway. He wasn't looking at me. His eyes were fixated on a point above me, out the grimy window, past the leaves that littered its sill, unblinking.

But before all that, before our relationship would evolve and deepen and become the defining one of our young, high-strung lives, James and I had left the glow of a bonfire to sit on the damp trunk of a recently dead tree and test each other with words.

"Tell me about your mom," I said.

"She was . . . stable," he said.

"Before she died?"

"No, stable as in . . . level. Really chilled out." He dragged deep on his cigarette, and words came tumbling out along with the curling smoke. "She wanted everyone to be comfortable and settled down and going about their business. She didn't like rocking the boat, not even when she got sick. It was like, they diagnosed it, and nothing changed except that there were all these pills in the bathroom cabinet all of a sudden. She wanted everything to be normal; she kept saying that things would be the same as always. She even got this wig, when she started losing her hair—it was exactly like her old hair. I mean, the same color and style and everything, and she'd have it on in the mornings and be standing there making coffee, like nothing was wrong."

"That's admirable," I said, not knowing what else to say.

"It just made it harder when things got bad," he said quietly. "And they did."

"Did what?"

"Get bad."

I waited to see if he'd say more. He started speaking again, still not looking at me. "My dad and I, we wanted to stop pretending and just deal with it. You know? Just talk about it. She kept saying no, nothing was wrong, except *everything was wrong*, and you could *see* it. Everything was completely off about her, she was so pale and skinny. She started walking in this weird way. Like it hurt her just to put one foot in front of the other. She used to go running all over the house, cleaning everything at once, trucking the vacuum cleaner up and down the stairs, and then all of a sudden she's shuffling around the kitchen like some old woman, and we're supposed to act like everything's fine." He sucked on his cigarette again. I kept silent.

"And that fucking wig," he continued, growing bitter. "I mean, she wasn't fooling anyone. It never even looked *close* to real. And she wouldn't let us talk about it. And then, at the end . . ."

He stopped.

I waited until I was sure that he was finished.

"But she was trying to make things easier on you, right?"

"I don't know," he said, and refused to look at me. "If that's what it was, it didn't work."

I leaned into him, trying to comfort him with the solid weight of my body against his. I felt warm with his confidence. Nobody had shared a tragedy with me before. His hand moved over and covered mine. We sat, not talking.

I was brushing my hair from my eyes, leaning against his shoulder while we shared yet another cigarette, thinking that maybe he'd kiss me soon, when I felt him stiffen.

"What?" I asked, drawing up.

"Ah, shit," he said, gesturing toward the fire, the damp reeds somebody had thrown on the blaze creating plumes of billowing smoke that climbed skyward and out over the treetops, over our heads. "What a bunch of assholes. You know how many summer people are going to see that from their back decks, freak out about forest fires, call the police?"

"How many?"

"One is all it takes."

"And then what?"

"And then we'll all be in deep shit."

"Should we go back?" I said, fidgeting.

"I guess *you* should," he said flatly, looking at me with something like contempt. "You wouldn't want to get caught out with someone like me if the police showed up, right? Honor student that you are, and all."

I hopped off the tree trunk, brushed moss from my behind, and zipped my sweatshirt. The good feeling that something shared and heavy was settling around us was gone. I felt flared-up and annoyed.

"Touchy," he said, smirking a little.

"Like you're not," I said. "I've been sitting here with you, having a perfectly nice time"—I winced at how snobbish I sounded, but continued—"but if you're going to act like an ass, forget it." I turned to go.

"Hey—"

"Forget it, James. Thanks for the cigarettes. I'm sorry about your mom."

I was halfway back to the fire when he caught up to me.

"Sorry," he said.

I shrugged.

"All right," I replied, still walking. I stepped quickly over a gaping maw in the ground, a marshy puddle so deep that it looked like a black hole. James hopped over it a moment after me.

"No, really," he said. "I didn't mean it that way."

I stopped walking, faced him, waited. He looked flushed, his cool-boy composure rattled.

"I just wanted to talk to you; I got nervous. You're the judge's daughter and everything."

I sighed. My father's profession, sitting on the bench in county court, caught up with me at the weirdest times.

"So we're cool now?" I said with exasperation.

"We're cool," he said, and fell silent. We stood in the dark.

The humming of a car motor and a quick siren, a one-note *buh-wip*, cut through the air.

"What'd I tell you," said James. He turned and started walking, quickly, back into the dark of the woods.

"Where are you going?" I asked, watching through the trees as the firelit crowd by the river turned, with expressions that ranged from full-out panic to resigned sheepishness, toward the police cruiser.

"Come on," he said, beckoning.

"Where are we going?"

"I'm taking you home," he said.

Twenty minutes later, he pulled carefully into my driveway. The house was dark. Surrounding us again were the sounds of nighttime, things that chirped and twittered, singing into the black, a song that would go on until dawn.

He circled the front of the truck, opened the door, extended a hand toward me. I swatted it away and hopped out unassisted.

"You think you're such a fireball," he said. His voice was husky. I laid my head against his chest, inhaling his scent as it mingled with the night air. Deodorant, soap, cigarette smoke, the light smell of his sweat—all rising from his skin and fusing with the heavy, rich scent of soil, the moist dew. The ethereal, muted tones of wild roses in the back garden. The sharp, sweet smell of alcohol.

And then I tilted my face toward his while his arms came up around me.

CHAPTER 4

*J*ames nodded at me through the grit-covered screen door, standing awkwardly on the front porch of the house, hands buried deep in his pockets. We had once spent an afternoon like this, on either side of the door, experimenting with the barrier it created.

"If I got sent to prison and you visited me, this is what it would be like," James had said. We were pressing our hands together on either side of the screen, the pads on our fingertips straining through the tiny holes.

"I don't think they have screens in prison," I replied.

"You know what I mean," he said, lunging forward with mouth open, moaning melodramatically. His lips pressed fleshily against the mesh.

"Now, *that's* disgusting," I said. "Do you know how long it's been since that thing was washed?"

"C'mon, baby," he said, his face straining, the tip of his

nose mashed against the side of his face. He moaned and grunted, the screen turning his tongue gray, painting dirty grid marks on his forehead, while I'd dissolved in laughter. "C'mon, let's make contact! I'm in for life, dammit, this is all I'll ever know of looooove!"

Now, as James stood uncomfortably on the porch, it seemed impossible that we'd ever been so unguarded.

I opened the door, stepped out, and closed it behind me.

"Hey," James said.

"Hey," I said, eyeing him.

He tried to meet my eyes and failed, looking instead at a spot of peeling paint, exposed wood, to the right of his foot. He looked like hell. His shaggy hair, always uncontrollable and mussed and flyaway, was matted in clumps. The skin on his face was gray and slack, sagging under his eyes and against his cheekbones, sinking into the pitted hollows above his jaw. His bloodshot eyes darted between my face and his own feet.

"I look like shit, right?" he said, smiling wanly.

I bit down against love, fought against moving toward him or touching him or asking if he was all right. I thought to myself, I *don't care, don't care, don't care,* until the thought had taken on a life of its own and beat with dull pulses against the inside of my skull. I didn't care. I would not care, refused to care.

His smile faded. "Okay, so let's talk."

"Let's go out back," I said. "Where it's more private."

James nodded. We walked, a foot of self-conscious space in between us, across the sunny lawn to the place where it suddenly dipped and gave way to a steep, rough incline studded with trees. At the bottom, only a couple feet deep and making inconspicuous babbling sounds, was a small creek. This was where we had always sat together, in lazy conversation, in the permanent shade of one enormous maple tree whose gnarled roots had pushed their way through the lawn in reaching, fingerlike knobs.

I settled against the tree. James paced nearby for a moment, then dropped to the ground in front of me. He picked at the dirt, collecting tiny stones and flinging them halfheartedly into the creek, while I waited.

"I don't know what to say," he said finally.

"How about, 'I'm sorry,'" I replied flatly.

"I—" he said. His voice cracked. "Of course I'm sorry. The last thing I'd ever want to do is hurt you."

I glared at him, willing myself to be hard-hearted. Tough. Unflinching in the face of contrition.

"That's funny. Because fucking and then dumping someone in the same fifteen-second period? I'd call that hurting."

He flinched at the word *fuck*.

"Please don't do that," he said.

"You don't get to tell me what to do," I snapped.

"It wasn't like that!" he cried.

"Then tell me what it was like, James. Tell me what happened. Tell me what *you* think happened in your truck last night. Because to me, it was pretty goddamn clear."

"I don't know. I don't know," he said. "Maybe I wasn't thinking."

"So what, it was instinctive?" My voice rose. "Is that

what you're saying? To get in my pants and get inside me and then just ditch me like some *thing*? Like a piece of trash?"

"No," he said, and stopped. He only managed to get out two more words—"I just—"—when his voice broke.

The sight of his wide-open face made my stomach clench.

James was crying, something I'd never seen him do. He had been close, once, the one and only time I had asked him about the day his mother died, when his voice had cracked and I had immediately regretted ever asking, had fallen down apologizing and begging him to pretend it had never happened. Now he was looking at me, finally, eyelids swollen with tears, red and wet and with only dark, oily slits where his iris showed between.

He swiped at his eyes, coughing, and then cleared his throat.

He said, "I was thinking, all right. I was thinking about everything."

I watched him regain control of himself, willing myself to stay silent.

"Everything," he said again. He gazed into the distance and kept talking. "I always knew you would leave, you know, at the end of the summer. I knew that you'd leave, and I'd still be here, and that'd be it."

"We never talked about that," I started, but he waved a hand to shut me up.

"Come on, Rebecca," he said. "You're dying to get out of here, you've said it a million times. I get that, you don't really fit in, or whatever it is. I thought you could've tried harder. But I just kept thinking about that, the whole time that you were on the stage, how everybody up there was moving on. Except for me. Tons of those kids are leaving town, but not me. I have to stay here."

"That's bullshit. You could have had your diploma this year. Hell, you could go back in the fall and be done in a semester," I said.

"But for what?" said James. "Where would I go? My dad can't send me anywhere. And I couldn't leave him alone."

I sighed. "He would understand."

"It wouldn't be right."

"No, it just wouldn't be easy."

He looked at me again. "Maybe. But . . . I was so pissed off, so angry. I didn't want that, to be here forever. Watching you up there, it made me feel like I've got no choice, and it made me so goddamn angry, and then you said that thing about being salutatorian and it was like a fucking slap in the face. Like you'd already moved on and left town, like I wasn't good enough for you anymore."

"Christ, James," I said, "it was a fucking joke."

"I know," he said.

"So, what, that's it? You just got pissed, and you decided to hurt me before I could hurt you?"

"I never wanted to hurt you."

"Well, you did."

We sat together, the rushing breeze making rustling sounds in the trees, the branches above our heads creaking, groaning, moving in time with the wind. The air was thick with the scent of wild roses.

So thick, that smell. It stifled, pressed back against

the golden thrust of the sun. The wild rose wants to be remembered, wants to color the afternoon with its heady essence, so that every summer recollection is tinted with its sweet, soft-petaled scent. It was a blanket that covered everything, crept into my nose and flooded my eyes with perfume that couldn't be blinked away.

The heat, the same heat that had tormented the police that morning as it stripped down the dead girl and urged her stiff, dry flesh into baking decay, was beating against my skin. It was crushing. I wanted to succumb, let it force me prostrate against the ground. It wrapped wetly around my sweating thighs and blew against the beads that trickled down my forehead. It soaked James's shirt with perspiration, sticking it against his ribs and under his arms.

Sitting there, making heavy indentations in the thirsty grass, we looked at each other and wondered who would collapse first.

"Listen," he said. I kept my eyes on him.

"We can wait it out," he said. "No pressure, no expectations. Whatever you want, whatever feels right to you, that's what we'll do. But . . . but I was wrong. I don't want this to end."

"I'll be gone," I said. "I'm going."

The words felt hollow. The thick and faraway voice didn't sound like mine.

"That's what you should do," James said, so forcefully that it startled me. "But we can still have this summer, can't we? I want to make this up to you."

I shook my head. "I don't—"

"Becca, at least let me try. Wouldn't you rather have it that way? You leaving, and thinking that last night was really who I am, that's what I can't stand."

Looking at him, my stomach churned. He had hurt me, pulled the rug from under me, knocked my breath away so swiftly and abruptly that I thought I might never get it back. I tried to focus. To care only for myself, to think about last night. Its reality, its physicality.

The smell of the grass.

The sound of his breathing.

His voice, floating down from the ambiguous dark overhead, saying, "This is done."

Instead, as he looked at me, waiting, I felt my conviction falter.

What happened had been shocking. It had hurt. But it wasn't supposed to happen that way.

I wasn't ready to let go.

James moved toward me, the grass sighing and springing back with relief from his weight, and cupped my face with one of his hands.

"I love you," he said. "I'm sorry. I love you."

Nothing moved.

I held my breath.

James held my hand and looked past me, his eyes unfocused and far away.

He said, "It's going to be okay."

I awoke an hour later with my head resting heavily on his chest. In the moments that followed our conversation, I was suddenly, crushingly exhausted. I had fallen asleep almost instantly, cushioned by the soft grass at the base of the maple tree, to the feeling of his fingers in my hair.

I sat up, hot and disoriented in the muted pink light. Behind me, the sun was creeping toward the horizon.

"How long was I out?"

James looked down at his chest and said, "Long enough to drool. A lot."

"Oh," I said. I felt awkward and unsure of myself. "Sorry." He smiled and shrugged, moving stiffly to his feet. A lightning bug flashed over his shoulder.

"Do you want to get dinner or something?" he asked. He shifted from one foot to the other, as though uncertain, in the wake of our last words, whether the relationship had changed completely. Where did we go from here? Forward? Backward?

"Not tonight."

He sighed. "Okay."

"This is . . . a lot."

"I understand."

He squatted down beside me, traced a finger along my temple. Gooseflesh broke out on my arms and legs at his touch.

"There's something I want to know," he said.

"What?"

"I understand that last night, what happened . . . well, that it was wrong. I understand why you feel the way you do. But after today, after what I told you, does it make any sense at all?"

His voice was pleading. I thought about James, his insecurity and his fear of being left alone, and about the night before—not how it ended, but how it began. I remembered the swish of polyester as each kid tripped awkwardly across the stage to shake the principal's hand, the sweaty grip, the diploma handoff. I remembered looking out, over the sea of audience members with upturned faces, perched on groaning folding chairs. I remembered seeing James, standing just behind the back row, with his hands deep in his pockets and his eyes fixed, unblinking, on each of his friends as they closed the high school chapter of their lives and shuffled back to their seats. He had felt the weight of stagnation, seen nothing ahead but a lifetime of desertion, friends who never came back, and day after day of unbearable small-town shit.

"Becca?"

"Yes," I said.

I understood.

CHAPTER 5

*E*arly on—after that first night at the bonfire, after our first and second and tenth kiss, when the sunset began coming earlier and the slow plod of summer gave way to the hectic reentrance of back to school—there had been a fight. Our first and only. For me, it had been resolved and forgotten. It was eclipsed by the deepening feelings that had turned out to be love.

It was different for James. I knew that, now. He had carried it with him for almost a year, nursing his grudge through the long cold of winter, holding it tightly while he watched me walk the stage at graduation, letting the resentment grow bigger and wilder until it burst out and knocked us both senseless.

I understood. I'd almost forgotten that once, it had been me who tried to end it.

I'd waited until the last minute, late in the day. It had been two weeks but felt like longer, our connection so deep and immediate that we'd fallen naturally into a state of constant togetherness. It had been so blissful and easy to just forget that this was going nowhere, that senior year loomed large ahead. Summer had seemed sure to go on forever.

We were sitting on a tiny strip of uneven beach by Silver Lake, sucking on the rough, icy ends of colored freeze pops. He'd brought a whole sleeve of them, all twelve colors, half melted in a cooler full of ice. I watched him eat and grinned. I liked to suck the sugar from them, playing vampire, watching the ice turn pallid and then biting it off in a freezing chunk that made my teeth sing. But James was methodical, patient. He'd take one and hold it, letting the warmth of his hands permeate the plastic, letting the sleeve turn floppy and the ice turn to half-melted sludge, then drink it down in a shot. Two, maybe three gulps.

"I'm off on Monday," he said. He had been working construction that summer, sweating out the days on roadside duty, waving traffic through a single-lane choke with an orange hard hat and garish sign that said STOP on one side, SLOW on the other. One day, when I'd had nothing to do, I had driven out to Route 128 and U-turned back and forth along that one-lane pass five times, making faces while he tried not to laugh.

On my last pass-through, I'd flashed him.

Even on the smudged surface of my rearview mirror, I could see his mouth—morphing from gaping shock to a slow grin as I drove away.

"Oh, yeah?" I said.

"I could pick you up. You know, after school."

I laughed and dodged, saying, "You sound like my dad."

He didn't smile back.

He asked again, "So I'll come get you, then? I can meet you out front."

I didn't answer, began to fidget as the silence stretched five seconds too long. Then ten. Then: "Listen, James—" was all I managed before he jumped, sinking his teeth into the spot where I'd paused to take a breath.

"Never mind. Forget it," he said. The words came out clipped, short, wounded. I cringed at the sudden distance, but pressed on.

"No," I said. "We should probably talk about this. I mean, school's starting, and we—"

"No, really," he interrupted again, standing up abruptly and dropping a wrapper still half full of purple slush between us. "That's fine. You don't need to spell it out."

The sun had dipped below the tree line; behind us, the long, lean trunks of the evergreens cast vertical shadows on the water. They made me think of bars, of barriers. Of what might happen if I lingered too long by the lake with this boy who was beautiful and intense and going absolutely nowhere.

"It's not that I don't like you," I said, trying to keep my voice neutral. I wasn't lying; I did like James, liked him more than I'd ever liked the handful of other guys I'd semi-dated over the past couple years. They were like me—debate team members, scholar athletes, aspiring doctors. Guys who had plans, like I did, to escape through college and emerge on the other end into a bigger, better world. It was a mystery to me that the quiet resolve of my skinny summer fling could make these guys, with their serious plans, seem so shallow and one-dimensional.

But that's what he was: a summer fling. Not meant to last.

"But I'm not boyfriend material," he finished. I looked at him, feeling guilty and transparent and exposed. And, just for a moment, feeling worse for what I'd always wanted.

"You'd be a great boyfriend," I said, testing the idea out loud and feeling surprised when it felt like the truth. "It's not about that. It's really not. It's not you, it's just . . ." I trailed off in the face of his withering glare; the cliché died on my lips. I coughed and looked down, feeling my cheeks flush.

I wished that I'd waited until later, until nightfall, so that I could have made my pitch—an easy separation, faultless and early, disentangling ourselves from the mess of things before either of us could get hurt—in the safe, insulated cocoon of the dark. Then I wouldn't have had to see the open disappointment in his face.

My gaze settled on the ground, instead. The earth was in motion, boiling with ants, a mass of red bodies treading and tumbling over one another in their frantic rush for the spilled sugar near my feet. My stomach lurched and I shut my eyes.

The sound of jingling keys made me open them. James was standing a few steps away, looking sulkily at the ground.

"I knew this was a bad idea," he said. He was fishing in his pocket, turning away. He had called it quits on the conversation. It was over before it began. I scrambled to my feet.

"Would you just wait a second?" I cried. I'd had a plan, an idea of how this would go. This was not it. This was all wrong.

"Wait? Wait for what?"

"I'm still talking!" Annoyance had gotten the better of me. I wanted the last word.

"Fine, but I'm done listening."

I threw my hands against my forehead in frustration. "You haven't listened at all! I haven't even said anything! Why are you so pissed off?"

He shook his head, looking over the water. "I'm not pissed off," he said. "I'm disappointed."

"Okay, now you really do sound like my dad."

It was an ill-timed joke, out before I could stop myself. His eyes narrowed and my smile disappeared.

"Okay, okay, I'm sorry," I backpedaled. "I just . . . I wanted to talk about this, that's all. And the last thing I want is for you to be all bitter, or angry at me. I just thought—"

"What?" he said, turning back to look at me. "That we had a Labor Day expiration date?"

I leveled my gaze back at him. Inhaled. Exhaled.

And then, against the urgings of detachment and common sense, allowed a small but insistent sense of possibility to gain hold—the one that kept me awake at night, thinking of him, long after he'd dropped me in my driveway and the red eye taillights of his truck had disappeared into the dark.

"Are you saying we don't?"

He shook his head and shrugged. I reached for his hand and tugged him back, drawing him down to sit beside me again. I thought he might fight it, might jerk back from my touch and let that last, deadly bit of distance fall into place, but he didn't.

For a minute, we sat without talking, watching the lake grow glassy in the last light of day, looking out toward the splash where a fish had surfaced and vanished in a bolt of silver scales. James lit a cigarette. A cool breeze came across the water, a harbinger of the coming fall—and, I thought, the one after it. It seemed far, far away.

"I meant it, when I said that it isn't you," I said, daring to look directly at him. "But I have plans. And they don't include this town. I'm going to graduate, and then I'm gone. I'm not staying here a second longer than I have to."

"But you do have to," he pointed out. "For the next twelve months."

"And that's why this makes me nervous."

He dragged deeply, then lifted his chin and blew a stream of smoke toward the sky. "This?"

"This, meaning, this." I gestured at the space between us.

Because *yes*, I thought, there was something there. "Twelve months is a long time, it's definitely long enough for this to get . . . complicated."

"Complicated?" said James.

"Would you stop that?"

I kicked a clod of dirt at him while he snickered, furious but relieved, at least, that the wounded look was gone from his face.

He held up his hands. "Okay, okay. I'm sorry."

"This is what I'm talking about, though," I said, folding my arms and glaring at him. "Do you get that? I don't know what you're thinking. It's been two weeks, we haven't had time for discussion. So I'm telling you now, if this is just some game to you, I don't have time to play it. And if it's not—"

"It's not," he said, and he looked at me with so much intensity that my knees went weak.

"Then . . . I don't know how this works," I said, feeling my face turning red. I began fumbling with the fringe on my shorts, thinking, *This is why this was a bad idea. Why this IS a bad idea, because love makes people stupid.*

"I like you a lot—" I finally sputtered.

"Yeah, I like you, too," he interjected, watching with amusement as I tried to play it cool.

"—but I don't want to be one of those girls," I finished. "You know, the ones who get all crazy and clingy and end up going to the community college 'cause they can't leave their high school sweethearts behind."

"Hey, Becca," he said. "I didn't say anything about

wanting you to stay. I didn't even say anything about us being together in another three months."

I looked at him out of the corner of my eye. "So now you're saying you think this won't last another three months?"

"Don't be an asshole."

A long time passed before he spoke again, licking his lips and false starting twice before finally putting the words together.

"I just think that this"—he gestured at the air, just as I'd done—"is a good thing. And that there's no reason to mess with it. I know you're leaving—I mean, I wouldn't try to get in the way of that. But in the meantime, we could have a great year. You know?"

I nodded.

Eyes wide open, I penciled him in for graduation day. I signed up to have my heart broken.

"Unless you're too cool to date the dropout," he added.

I cringed at the word, thinking of my parents' inevitable reaction. They hadn't pressed for details about the mysterious boy I was suddenly spending every day with, and I hadn't offered any, but the magic don't-ask-don't-tell policy couldn't possibly last much longer. "So you're really not going back to school?"

"Would you?"

"If I were you?" I said. "I don't know."

"I'll probably get my GED," he said.

I nodded. I didn't ask what would come next; he offered nothing further. He had no plans; I didn't encourage him to make any. In a way, I thought, maybe it even made James a safe choice. I was the person in motion. I had the control. I was the one with a future, visible in the distance. And no matter how attached I became to him, I knew, at the end, that he was attached to Bridgeton. He was part and parcel of this town. And my heart—which had always yearned for a bigger life, which had always been in love with leaving— would lead me away from him when the time came.

And though I'd felt guilty to think of it, the sense of having the upper hand stayed with me as we walked through the woods in the deepening twilight. He took my hand as the sun crept down and the world turned purple, looking back in the last light to the place where we'd just been. I quickened my pace, feeling the pull of momentum.

Now, peering back from the other side of graduation, at the moment when my longed-for bigger life was supposed to start, it all seemed alien—like something that had happened to somebody else. The quiet confidence, the utter surety, when each of us played our roles so well and everything felt right.

When he knew I'd be gone at summer's end.

When I knew he would never leave.

"I understand," I said again, and James nodded, looking toward the horizon, where the sun was disappearing. It was nearly gone, only a painfully bright sliver that burst through the tops of the faraway trees. When he spoke again, his eyes were still fixed on the fading light.

"Do you ever feel like this? Like you're just stuck?"

"I don't know, James. I always had a plan."

"Do you see yourself there?" he asked. "Can you picture it?"

I tried to. I tried to imagine myself at the state university where I would be enrolled come September, walking past the low, square buildings that held classrooms and dorm rooms and offices. I tried to imagine the crispness of autumn, leaves underfoot, the brilliant sky and New England breeze.

Instead, I felt only the grass under my hands and the pressing air—heavy, hot, and damp. The scent of the wild roses clung to everything, insistent, clouding my mind with thoughts of sweat, curling hair, humidity, and the darkening sky.

"Maybe it's just too hard to see a place that you haven't already been," I said.

"I can't see my future," said James, his voice barely a whisper. "I try to picture it, and I don't see anything at all."

Around us, in the trees, fireflies were beginning to light and float in search of mates. The last hint of pink had disappeared on the horizon, but the heavy heat persisted. It would be a hot night, the kind that fans and open windows would do no good for.

I thought of the dead girl, who would surely have been moved by now, taken from the dirt and moved to a cold place. Refrigerator cold. A place where the low temperature might stall the ebbing breakdown of her flesh long enough to find something, on her body or in her blood, that would explain her presence here, in our town, dead on the side of the road.

James put his arm around my waist and drew me in, ducking his head to kiss me on the temple.

"I'll see you tomorrow," he said.

"Good night."

The door slammed. The motor turned over, coughed, then roared. James saluted, two-fingered, a cigarette already dangling between his lips.

The truck pulled away, out of the driveway and down the road, the taillights growing small and faint in the deepening twilight. And just as I'd always done, as if nothing had changed, I watched until they were out of sight.

AMELIA

*L*uke was coming. Minutes ago, the phone had rung, his tenor-pitched voice in her ear telling her to wait on the curb. She surveyed her bedroom, scanning for any forgotten necessity, any essential object on the verge of being left behind. The small space seemed vast now, nearly empty, twin beds and college-issue pine furniture surrounded by a sea of tile. Shiny, pristine patches on the floor showed where a lamp had stood, where the desk had been. A perfect, dustless rectangle marked the place she had dropped her calculus textbook—months ago, the day she'd dropped the class—never to touch it again. She smiled at the memory of her father's face when she'd explained, in her careful way, that she had traded in abstract math and imaginary numbers for the true, tactile reality of human emotion. She would not study calculus anymore. She wanted to experience life.

She had discovered the theater in her senior year, fallen almost by accident into a small speaking role when the girl to whom it belonged had left school unexpectedly for a family emergency. With only a week to go before the performance, they only needed someone who could memorize the lines and blocking, do the job, and then stay out of the way. Her roommate, a vivacious and bossy girl playing one of the leads, thought of Amelia.

"Don't be ridiculous," she had said. "I can't act."

"You don't really have to," the roommate had cajoled her. "It's just recitation. Like, mindless automaton. It'll actually be better if you're not too emotional."

"Isn't there someone else who wants to do it?"

"Not really."

"I don't know."

"Ame, come on! Just try one thing that's out of your comfort zone, would you? Be bold! You'll have plenty of time to wear horrible, classic-cut skirt suits once you graduate."

Amelia had smiled. "All right."

She was meticulous, smart, a quick learner. She studied the lines, learned them by heart, attended a dress rehearsal where she moved from place to place according to the notes in the script and the director's jerky hand movements. Her character was, indeed, mindless—an ignorant woman whose narrow way of thinking would condemn her to a drab, atonal life, moving single-mindedly from point A to point B. Amelia felt the desperation of such an existence, a life lived with eyes closed.

———•———

On the night of the first performance, buoyed by the energy of the crowd and the thrilling sense of her own body, her physical self, owning and occupying the space of the stage, she could sense the cutting edge of her character's loneliness. Her performance was tinted with it, imbuing the role with surprising depth. The director approached her that night.

"Thank you for stepping in. You did well," he said.

"Thank you for . . . having me," she said solemnly. He smiled and raised an eyebrow. She blushed and added, "Er, in the play."

"It was a pleasure," he said, still smiling.

She began to blush harder. He clapped her jovially on the shoulder and began to walk away, then looked back toward her.

"If you decide to keep it up, I can recommend a class or two," he said, looking carefully at her. Her eyes widened.

"Really?"

His smile became a wide grin. He was, she realized, amused by her.

"You're only in college once," he said.

She saw Luke later that night, when she slipped elatedly into his room with a six-pack of beer. He had missed the performance, begging the need to study for an early exam the next morning. He was sitting at his desk, highlighter in hand, still wearing the collared shirt and chinos he'd adopted as his going-to-class uniform. His posture was rigid, his eyes focused intently on the textbook in front of him. He was the picture of a future businessman—her future businessman. She stifled a laugh as she realized that he hadn't even unbuttoned the top of his shirt. He looked up at the sound.

"Madame Butterfly?" he said, his voice rising unnaturally.

"Not quite," she said, grinning. She turned a pirouette, placing the beer on his dresser with a flourish, then leaped toward him and swooped in to kiss him on the mouth. Instead of returning the kiss, he turned from her quickly with a pained smile, causing her to catch a mouthful of ear. She mock-spat.

"Yuck! Hey, what's with you?" she asked.

"Nothing."

"Luke, you just cold-shouldered me. What's up?"

He sighed, pulled her toward the bed, gestured for her to sit beside him. He draped his arm over her shoulders. She looked at him, questioningly. He looked back with knitted brows.

He bit his lip and then said, "You just seem awfully excited tonight."

"What, you mean, because of the play?"

"Well, that must be it, right? I've never seen you so worked up before; you're all flushed."

"Oh, well of course I am, dummy," she said, smiling. "It was an amazing experience, and I'd never done anything like this before."

"I know."

"But that doesn't explain why you're mad at me, all of a sudden."

"I'm not mad, Ame." He ran his fingers through his close-cropped hair. "I'm just surprised. I thought this was a favor you were doing for Christine; you didn't even seem that excited about it. And then you come in here, acting all crazy—"

"I am not acting crazy!"

"—when I've just been sitting here studying all night, alone."

"Is that what this is about? You're upset that I left you alone to study?"

He looked sheepish.

"That's not totally it," he said. "Obviously, we don't have to be together every second."

"Well, what is it?"

"It's just that you seem so happy. One week rehearsing, and one night onstage, and it's like somebody set you on fire."

"It does feel a little bit like that," she said.

"And this was your only performance, right? You were probably great, and I didn't even get to see it." He ran his fingers through his hair again, his lower lip protruding in a little-boy pout. She looked at him, loving him in spite of his ridiculous behavior, and patted his cheek.

"Awww," she said.

"So now I feel like a jerk," he continued. "My girlfriend was onstage for the first and only time in her life, and I was stuck back here with my nose in a book."

She sat, quiet, feeling the finality of those words—first and only. Her silence unnerved him. He looked sharply at her.

"Why do you look like that?"

"I was just thinking," she said, wary and measuring her tone against his mood. "I was thinking, maybe it won't be the only time."

"You're going to take up acting?" he said, looking almost incredulous. She felt her temper, usually dormant beneath her patient nature, flare up. He had pronounced the word, *acting*, in a sneering, indignant tone that made it sound like some sort of filthy habit.

"I'm not 'taking up' anything, Luke." Her voice was hard. "People study this, you know. Just because it's not hard science, just because it doesn't lead to a high-paying job at a hedge fund after college, doesn't mean it's not worth pursuing."

He shook his head. "I don't get it."

"What's not to get? I've found something I enjoy doing. I want to do more of it before I graduate, before I lose the opportunity. Why are you against that?"

His look softened. He touched her hand. "I'm not against it," he said. She looked at him with narrowed eyes. "I'm not," he said again. "I just thought, maybe you were having a hard time with senior year, or getting hung up about what would happen after graduation. You're on a good track, Ame. I don't want to see you sabotage yourself on a whim, just because you're worried about how things might pan out in the real world. I'm trying to look out for you."

"You make it sound like I'm going through some kind of phase."

"All I'm saying is, sometimes people get nervous when the rest of their lives are looming on the horizon. But if you just want to do a little soul-searching . . ." He trailed off.

"If you want to call it that, all right," she said. "But my mind's made up, regardless."

He sighed.

"All right, so what will you do? Join some kind of club, or something?"

"No," she said. "Joining a club, that just sounds trivial. I'm serious about this, and I only need one finance class to finish my major. I'm going to drop calc, do theater instead."

Two days after her college graduation, less than one before the tires of Grant Willard's truck would shatter her fingers into splintered dust on the roadside, she stood by the window in her empty room. The sense of something changing, of a different life stirring and awakening and unfolding its untested legs, gripped her with feverish intensity. The moment of discovery had passed; she had taken hold of it, her eyes opening to all of life's limitless possibilities, and now, as she sat in her empty room and waited for Luke, anticipation filled her with the urgent need to go, go, go.

On the street below, a nondescript white sedan pulled

carefully to the curb. Luke, squinting toward the sky from behind his glasses, emerged and looked up at her window. Amelia looked down at him, waiting for her, then gathered her single bag and rushed from the room in one, breathless movement. He was here, and she was ready.

She was on her way.

CHAPTER 6

*I*n a small town, murder is three-dimensional. We make it that way, elevating it and turning it over until it's more than a simple tragedy, until it becomes tangible. Murder in a small town is always more than a paragraph in the local paper. In a place so insulated, where lives are so small and gone about so quietly, violent death hangs in the air—tinting everything crimson, weaving itself into the shimmering heat that rises off the winding asphalt roads at noon. It oozes from taps and runs through the gas pumps. It sits at the dinner table, murmuring in urgent low tones under the clinking of glassware.

The shocking death of Amelia Anne Richardson was not Bridgeton's first. Years before, when I was still young enough that the summer passed in an endless, barefoot tumble of long afternoons, the *ftz-ftz-ftz* of sprinklers and tall glasses filled with cloyingly sweet iced tea, a woman named Sarah DiStefano shot her husband in their kitchen. Robert DiStefano, age forty-two, was dead before he hit the floor. He had been scanning the open refrigerator in search of beer, bent double with his hands resting on his knees and his considerable gut hanging, pendulous, between his straining and out-of-shape thighs. The bullet entered at the base of his skull as he peered into the space between a half-full bottle of ketchup and a foil-covered casserole. He was looking for a can of Coors Light and trying, vaguely, to recall whether it was in 1992 or 1993 that he'd last been able to touch his toes.

The day that news broke, murder was the breeze that whipped through Bridgeton's streets and the unseasonable chill that rose off the lake to tap its misty fingers against the windows. Neighbors tossed it back and forth over fences; children kicked it around in the street. It brought people together over coffee and at the gas pumps. It spewed from the mouths of the East Bank Tavern's beer-swilling Saturday crowd.

In a small town, everyone has inside information. If you asked around, you couldn't find a single person who didn't know either Sarah, the confessed murderess, or Robert, the unwitting victim. And with both of them gone—one dead, one sure to pass the rest of her years behind bars—there was nothing for it: Whether serving time or dead and buried, Sarah and Robert DiStefano no longer belonged. They were outsiders.

"I knew there was something weird about her," people said.

"Maybe he had it coming," they said.

It didn't matter if it was true. Out of the mouths of Bridgeton's remaining residents, each scattered anecdote or snap judgment was a fact, an explanation, a final insight into these people who had lived among us, certainly, but who had never truly fit in. To hear them talk, the DiStefanos had fooled no one.

Because he was a lech, a drunk. He was lazy. He would steal the cash from her purse, take it and go out all night, piss it away on booze or stuff it into a stripper's G-string. He'd run that woman ragged, wrung the life out of her. He'd slept around. She caught him with her sister, her best friend, with a woman named Tiffany, Tammy, or Sheena, a woman who lived in a trailer park twenty miles west of here. He beat his wife, berated her, broke her heart. He was lucky he'd lived as long as he did. He was lucky that he found a woman who'd put up with his shit for a few years, even if she put a bullet in his head at the end. It was his fault.

Or hers.

Because she never fit in. She was odd, nervous, twitchy. She was abrasive. She was too shy. She had jumpy eyes. Or not jumpy, exactly, but eyes set too close together— eyes that said she was capable of meanness, of insanity, of creating chaos with a single flick of her index finger. She was a shrew. She was a witch. She was never satisfied, not with him, not with this town. She heard voices. She took medication. Or didn't take it enough.

We knew this, all of us, because we'd been told by someone who knew. We knew it. Don't repeat it, don't say

I told you, but that's the truth. He had it coming, and there was always something weird about her.

The real events that led to Robert's death in the kitchen that night—the passing years in which Sarah became increasingly unstable, her struggle to fight it, the pains she'd taken to hide it from her loving but oblivious husband, and her final decline as she became convinced that her husband had been replaced by someone else, a stranger who meant her harm—they didn't matter. Nor did it matter that the rest of Sarah's life would play out not in prison, but quietly, her awareness dimmed to a bare glow by medication while she sat in a white-walled psychiatric hospital in a Boston suburb. We may not have known that, but we knew them. And we knew that they didn't belong here.

Buoyed by that knowledge, with the murder slowly migrating away from the paper's front page, with the story bleeding and seeping further and further back until it vanished entirely into the past, the people of Bridgeton drew close together.

And so, like murders before it, Amelia's murder was three-dimensional in its aftermath. It blew alongside the flecks of bloodstained dirt, down County Road 128, and reached town as a howling gale. The chatter was fevered. Frenzied. People came home from the grocery store, from bridge club, from a walk in the park, and massaged jaw joints that were exhausted from gossiping. They stood over fences and talked about the dead girl, the girl with no name, no face, no identification.

But as people talked, they became uneasy. In their

vernacular, there was no anonymous death. They had no facts to share, no stories to compare. Nobody knew the victim, and more than that, nobody knew who had killed her. People remembered the death of Robert DiStefano. Thinking of its aftermath, they decided that that sort of murder was preferable—the sort where the names and places and hard facts were all in place. Where everybody knew the players and the plot. After all, it was things like that, those small-town tragedies, that really brought a community closer together.

An anonymous death in a small town, that's a different thing. It makes people uneasy. They stop gossiping, talk only with trusted friends, or—realizing that nobody can truly be trusted—they don't talk at all. Instead of settling in the streets or running through the municipal sewer system, murder moves inside. It becomes internalized. It seeps around the corners of locked front doors. It creeps into people's bedrooms. It runs in their veins.

People sit on their porches, they smoke, they look with narrowed eyes down the darkened streets and into their neighbors' windows. Inside, murder tiptoes up the back stairs and hides behind a bedroom door.

The people, alone on their porches or gathered quietly around the kitchen table, consider the unknowns. They form theories. They wait for information. And when they go inside, upstairs, when the lights go out and they lie, wakeful, in their beds, they wonder if everything has changed.

CHAPTER 7

I'm fine.

I repeated this to myself as I sat in my car, putting on makeup, wearing black. Black shirt, black pants, black apron: the required uniform at the bistro that had been my after-school job, where I now waitressed Wednesdays through Saturdays. The driver's-side visor was flipped down, its mirror open, reflecting the bags under my eyes and a healing zit on my forehead. I smeared my lips with gloss.

It was my first shift since summer began, a week since the night that left me watching James disappear down the road. A week since I'd found myself alone again, standing in the yard with a headache and his words, *We can still have this summer,* echoing insistently behind him.

I had walked toward the warm glow of my house, yellow light behind wavy glass windows, safe and bright and with family inside. The screen door had slammed behind me. My mother had called my name.

"Do you want dinner?"

My tongue was coated with wool, cottony in my mouth. It had grown hair. The inside of my mouth had never been drier. My stomach was empty.

I walked into the kitchen where she sat, eating from a white container of Chinese food. Gluey fried rice rode the fork to her mouth. The sight of the food, the grease spots on the tablecloth, and the chunks of artificially colored pork made my throat twitch with nausea.

"I don't think I want any of that," I said.

"Well good, because I'm not giving you any," my mom replied, taking another forkful and winking at me. "Your father is late, and I wasn't sure if you'd be here for dinner or not. Did James go home?"

"Yeah," I said, thinking, *Please don't ask anything else*, and thinking, too, *Please, ask me what happened*.

"Okay. So, dinner?" she asked again.

I went to the table and sat down with a sigh. A half-full bottle of red wine sat in the spot across from her, as though it had found the seat available and decided to take my dad's place. Looking at the dreamy look on my mother's face, I thought that might not be far from the truth. I reached for it.

Other times, my hand would have been swatted away. Instead, Mom just watched with a half smile as I grabbed the bottle by its neck and brandished it, threatening to drink from it.

"That's what you want?"

"Maybe I feel like drinking." It was the truth. Not only that, but the thick scent of the wine had wakened my stomach. Its protesting clench, its strike against food, had subsided.

Mom giggled. I was pretty sure that I knew where the top half of the bottle's liquid had disappeared to.

"Well?" I said, sloshing it at her.

She looked out the window for a second, toward the garden and the hidden incline where James and I disappeared a few hours earlier, and smiled again.

"You're an adult, right? High school graduate? I think you deserve a drink."

"What? Really?"

"Just get yourself a glass, would you? I don't want you stumbling around the kitchen with your lips wrapped around that thing like some kind of hobo." She giggled again.

"All right." I tried to hide my surprise as I grabbed a long-stemmed goblet from the cabinet above the sink. No doubt my mother knew that this wasn't my first drink, but to this point, she and my father had done a good job of pretending my innocence; all I'd had to do was nod, play along, and avoid vomiting in the rosebushes on the nights that I came home wasted.

I sat down again, filled the glass, and took a long sip while my mother grinned at me.

"Nice," I said. "Do most hobos drink Pinot Noir?"

"Ha!" she said.

"What?"

"I thought you were going to say, 'Do most hobos drink *pee!*'" She cackled through a mouthful of fried rice.

By the time I teetered off to bed, we'd been sipping for hours, laughing at nothing, until the past twenty-four hours felt like nothing but a hazy, bad dream. Two bottles of wine were empty—drained but for the deep red silt that ringed the depression in their heavy bottoms—my father had come home, and although I didn't feel particularly adult, at least I could sleep. My head thudded heavily on the pillow and I swallowed hard, trying to combat my body's insistence that the room had begun to spin. I was dead asleep within moments, oblivious to the heat or the noise of the katydids. I didn't hear the voices that carried from the kitchen, my mother's tone raised and shrill.

And now, I was fine.

Almost.

I had zombie moments; I sat for hours, staring at my college packing list, too paralyzed to even touch my sock drawer. At night, I would stare unfocused at the cordless phone—waiting for his inevitable call, but yelping when the chirruping ring shattered the silence. I had begun to move at half pace, trying to keep steady, trying to keep moving at all.

If things had been normal, someone might have seen my raw eyes and slack expression and asked me whether everything was okay.

But nobody did—not my friends, not my family, not the head chef at the restaurant outside of which I sat and stared at my own pallid reflection. I was temporary. I had a sell-by date, good only until the end of the summer. My dark moods, my nervousness, my paralysis in the face of the future—they were all understandable. If I seemed to be fading, they thought, it was only natural. I was on my way out, moving on, already gone.

The dead girl on the side of the road had yet to be identified; with the question of who she was and how she came to be there still hanging in the air, the almost-ghost that I was attracted no attention.

The visor snapped shut under my hand. The car door slammed behind me.

I had always liked waitressing: the constant movement, folding napkins and filling drink orders, the hours flying by while I paced the dining room. But tonight, I couldn't concentrate. Knives slipped through my fingers and left gouges on the floor. Tables full of summer people, giddy and boozy at the three-day reprieve of the Fourth of July, laughed and smiled beatifically when I forgot to bring bread or beer. One woman even patted my arm, saying, "Don't you worry, dear—I'm sure you'll be off to school soon anyway."

Halfway through my shift, I stood up too suddenly in the busy kitchen and dropped a full bottle of ketchup on the dirty tile. It shattered, splattered, shards of cheap glass with a viscous red coating skittering across the floor and under the sinks.

Tom, the chef, clapped me jovially on the shoulder and left a five-fingered grease stain on my shirt.

"Ten points!" he called.

"I'm sorry," I said. I licked ketchup off my finger.

"Hey, I understand," he said, waving a hand at me. He smelled like garlic and sweat. "You were thinking about some boy, yeah?"

"Sure," I said.

"I bet!" He winked. "Well, there you go. Everybody's gotta break one thing before they leave."

My occasional forays into the world of the living dead had sapped my conversation skills. I couldn't banter or chitchat—not with Tom, not with the dishwasher, not with the cashier at the XtraMart who would charge me $1.25 for a Coke on my way home. I muttered something about having gotten it out of the way.

"Ah, yeah," he said again. "I understand! And don't you worry about that ketchup, one of the boys will clean that up. Don't wanna send you off with a nasty cut. Travel healthy!"

"I've got a few more weeks," I said, but it was lost in the clatter of pans and the hiss of steam as the kitchen moved to life again. Tom, a good guy, a handsome man who flirted with the older waitresses because he knew that it made them feel good, was already handing a mop to the guy who washed the dishes.

"You get that, Manny, will ya?" he said, and turned back to the stove. He clapped the lid onto a pan with a resounding clang.

"You guys hear about that girl?" he announced, to no one in particular.

There was a chorus of "What?" from every corner of the kitchen. Nobody said, *which girl*. Everyone knew who he was talking about.

I grabbed a new bottle of ketchup, skirting the broken glass as I turned to leave.

"Still no idea who she is," Tom said. "But I heard something, from a guy who knows one of those cops. You know what he said? Said they think somebody came in and messed around, screwed things up in the crime scene."

"Somebody like who?" said Manny.

As I slipped through the swinging door to the dining room, Tom's voice floated after me.

"Dumb kids, probably," he said. "They do stupid shit like that. Walk all over things. They don't think."

The door closed behind me.

CHAPTER 8

When the time had come, I hadn't looked at political science programs, or Greek life, or student body size. I ignored all of that, the picking and choosing, the quick criteria they said would help me to narrow down my overwhelming field of potential futures. Instead, I took a map of New England and a compass, set its piercing metal leg on the black dot of Bridgeton, and drew a wide, red circle around everything within a two-hundred-mile radius.

"What's that?" my father had said, looking over my shoulder at the bleeding arc, the towns and counties now hidden under a thick, dark ribbon of ink. When I lifted the compass, I saw that it had marred the paper—a stab through the small, black heart of my hometown—and smiled.

"That," I said, "is everywhere I'm not going."

"Planning your escape, are you?" he grinned back, then pointed at a larger dot on the map. "But what about

Boston? That's a nice, big city, and an easy trip home on the weekend."

I shook my head. "It's not about living in a city."

It wasn't. Back then, it wasn't just about getting away. It was about not coming back. It wasn't just the size and sensibility of this place that made it unbearable, but its pull—the weird magnetism that could sap your ambition, clip your wings, leave you inert and fascinated and sinking ever deeper into the choking quicksand of small-town life. I'd seen it happen, how hard it was to get out. Every year, one or two kids would visit from college for a long October weekend and simply never leave. They came home, cocooned themselves in the familiar radius of the town limits, and never broke free again. Years later, you'd see them working in the kitchen at the pizza place, or sitting at the bar in the East Bank Tavern. Shoulders hunched, jaw set, skin slack. And in the waning light of their eyes, the barest sensation that once upon a time, they'd been somewhere else . . . or maybe it was only a dream.

When I found myself home at the end of the day, with nowhere to go and nothing to do, I would look in the mirror and see that same dimmed-out dream, losing its luster somewhere behind my own eyes.

Inside the house, the atmosphere was heavy with things undiscussed: Dad's continued absences in the evening, the empty bottles that seemed to appear overnight in our trash bin, the lines that formed around my mother's eyes. The dead girl was there, too—she had taken up residence in our house and in my head, drifting in from her resting place on the side of the road to look over my shoulder. At night, I would sometimes dream of her—that she was there with me, head resting gently on the pillow, staring at the ceiling with eyes like peeled grapes, whispering a gravestone verse from one of the monuments in our town's old boneyard.

Stop and think as you pass by, she hissed. *As you are now, so once was I.*

She was. She had been. She had died that night, less than a mile from the wide-open field where I'd parked with James. She had died, probably, just as I had gone to sleep. I lay awake and stared into the dark. I wondered who had killed her, whether she'd known him, loved him. Whether he'd loved her.

Not all of the empty bottles in our trash belonged to my mother. I had gotten a taste for cheap red wine, the heavy, grapy stuff that my parents uncorked at parties once everyone was too drunk to appreciate something more refined.

The crunch of gravel in our driveway alerted me to James's arrival, and I padded down the stairs. In the kitchen, my father was shaking his head with trademark disapproval.

". . . a real piece of work," he was saying. "Gave the chief a bunch of attitude and wouldn't let anyone in. They had to come back with a warrant, just to search the damn yard."

"James is here," I said.

"Call us if you'll be out late," my mother said, her voice tired, without looking up.

James leaned against the truck, arms folded, as I slipped out the front door and waved with a nonchalance I didn't feel. My hand floated through the hot, hazy air.

"What's up?" I asked, padding across the thirsty grass to stand in front of him.

"Party tonight at Craig's place," he said. "Want to come?"

"I haven't seen you in more than two weeks," I said, folding my arms to mimic his stance. "This is what you want to do tonight?"

"I thought it might be better for you. Ease back into it, sort of."

I snorted. "Being around Craig doesn't exactly relax me."

James looked hurt. "I'm trying, Beck. We don't have to go. I just thought it could be fun."

I touched his forearm.

"Hey," I said. "Sorry. I know you're trying."

"You don't have to decide right now."

We drove out of town instead, weaving from asphalt to curb as James fishtailed through the rough gravel, brick-colored dust that had scattered itself over the road in tiny, hastily rolled dice. I barely noticed. Moments earlier, I had reached into the glove compartment, looking for cigarettes, and instead pulled out a filthy bandanna stained with what looked like blood.

"What the fu—" I'd started, then yelped as James's hand suddenly slammed the compartment closed. "Hey!"

"What were you doing?"

"I wanted to *smoke*," I said, exasperated. I held up the bandanna. "What the hell is this? Is this yours?"

He looked at me for a long time—too long—then sighed and refocused his gaze on the road.

"James?"

"It's mine," he said.

I waited for an explanation, but none came. I watched James grinding his teeth and realized that the scenery outside had blurred, that the truck was beginning to rattle as his foot grew heavier on the pedal.

"I'm not proud of it, okay. But that night, after . . ." He looked uncomfortable for a moment, then swallowed and spat out the words, "I punched out a window."

"What?" Disbelief made my voice rise in a sharp-pitched crescendo. "What the hell? Why would you do that?"

The discomfort deepened; he squirmed in his seat and wouldn't look at me.

"I was . . . I don't know. I wasn't thinking very clearly, you know? I just felt angry and I wanted to break something."

I shook my head. "Apart from my heart, you mean."

He looked wounded; I felt simultaneously stupid and helpless. I couldn't seem to stop bringing up that night, tossing it out like a grenade whenever things started to feel normal again. As though he needed reminding of what he'd done.

"Sorry," I muttered. "Shitty joke."

He stayed quiet for a long time.

"I wish you wouldn't do that," he said, finally. "I wish . . . I wish you *couldn't*. I wish I could go back and make everything about that night disappear."

The truck swerved around another turn, hugging the road this time. James's mouth kept twitching, little creases forming and unforming at the corners where cheek met lip.

"So I guess they have a suspect or something," I said, finally, changing the subject. "For the mystery girl? My dad was saying something about some guy, and a warrant."

James shook his head too quickly, a dismissive motion that never failed to set my teeth on edge.

"It's not a suspect."

"Oh yeah? How can you be so sure?"

He coughed.

"Because it's Craig."

My jaw dropped.

"What?! They think he—"

"It's not like that," he interrupted. "That space, just back from the road, that's his property. Or his grandmother's. But he's the one there, so . . . I don't know, the cops just wanted to search it for evidence, like, if something blew over there—"

"And he wouldn't let them," I finished. "That's what my dad was saying. He told them to go get a warrant."

James shrugged. "He's allowed."

"He's *allowed*?" I cried. "He's an asshole! What if there was something there, evidence or something? And," I added, suddenly remembering, "I heard someone saying that the cops think the scene was tampered with."

James stiffened in the driver's seat.

"You heard *who* saying that?"

"Um . . ." I looked down at the floor and muttered, "Tom."

"What?"

"*Tom*," I said, exasperated. "At the restaurant."

His posture relaxed again. "Okay, and what does Tom know about anything?"

"I don't know. The cops go in there, all the time. I'm sure he hears things."

He looked at me, sidelong and with skepticism, emphasizing each word to make it sound ridiculous. "He. Hears. Things."

"Stop being a jerk. Just tell me, really—they're investigating Craig?"

"No," he said slowly, as though talking to a toddler. "They're investigating Craig's *yard*."

"Oh my God."

"What?"

I folded my arms, stewing, and looked out the window.

"Rebecca," said James. "Hey, Becca, come on."

I clenched my teeth together so hard that they squeaked. James made an exasperated sound.

"All right, yes. Okay? If it makes you feel better to say it that way, they're investigating Craig."

"Wonderful."

"But anyway," he continued, "it's just a technicality. If

there was something important back there, something that might help, then it wouldn't have taken them two weeks to get around to searching."

"In another town, I'd agree with you in a heartbeat."

"Oh, no faith in the hard-working men of the Bridgeton Police Department?"

"I'm sure they're doing the best they can, but how on the ball do you think they are? It's not like they have practice."

"They're getting help," he said. "And they've had murders before."

"Not like this."

James waved a dismissive hand and fell silent, chewing his lip. Outside, fields full of high-growing, starved yellow grass blurred by as the truck rumbled past. The brittle stalks waved and snapped, thirsty, straining toward the sky in search of rain that hadn't come for weeks.

I was quiet for a minute, thinking about Craig—smug, superior Craig. So convinced that in our drab little town, his seasonal residency and California birth certificate gave him the inalienable right to say, do, *take* whatever he wanted.

"I just don't think your asshole friend should be doing things that make their lives harder."

James sighed, exasperated.

"I'm tired of talking about this. You need to let it go," he said.

"Why?" I snapped. "If he has nothing to hide—"

"Becca," he said, so sharply that the rest of the sentence died instantly before reaching my lips. "Enough."

We drove in silence, until the sun was nearly gone. The last light in the sky was dusky, purple. James turned the truck onto County Road 128 and headed toward the mountains.

"Becca, I just don't want to talk about it. The dead girl, the investigation, any of it. I just want to focus on this summer, I want us to start fresh, and that means focusing on us. Just us."

The exhaustion in his voice was palpable, and I felt suddenly ashamed. He was doing everything he could to make things right, and I was doing everything I could to hold us back.

"I'm sorry," I said, finally. "I understand."

"Okay. Will you give me that rag, now?"

I was still clutching it, creasing it with the heat from my clenched fist.

"Why?" I asked uneasily, but handing it over.

James tucked the bandanna into his pocket and rolled his eyes.

"Because I want to hold your hand."

AMELIA

*H*e drove them north, up the turnpike and then through the Holland Tunnel, until they were deep in the crawling traffic of Chinatown. Outside the window, the scenery shifted—from far-off oil refineries whose insectlike steel structures towered over the landscape, to the immediate grit and dirt and noise of the city. She looked at Luke's pinched expression, more squinty with each passing minute, and tried not to laugh.

As they sat in the crowded thoroughfare of Canal Street, the light turned red and the cars ceased moving.

"You okay over there?" he asked.

"Yes," she said.

"You're being pretty quiet."

"I'm enjoying the ride."

Outside the car, pedestrians swarmed and tumbled

through the street. They jostled for position on curbs, endlessly moving in and out of stores whose high walls were covered with cheap T-shirts, gold jewelry, knockoff handbags, mugs and postcards and shot glasses with renderings of the Empire State Building or Statue of Liberty.

"You haven't asked what we're doing here," Luke said.

"Didn't I?"

"No."

"Oh." She paused. "I wasn't thinking about it, I guess."

Luke made an exasperated snort.

"What?"

"It's nothing," he said. "Just that you've been off in la-la land ever since graduation. I mean, I take a detour into New York and you don't even ask what's up? You're a million miles away. It's weird."

"I was . . ." She had already said, enjoying the ride. "I just wasn't concerned."

"You weren't concerned, or you weren't paying attention?"

She smiled at him, reached for his hand. He'd always been an antsy driver, had always been prone to picking fights in the car. She had found it infuriating at times, but today, she seemed to have a limitless well of patience and understanding for Luke's little idiosyncrasies. He let her intertwine her fingers with his.

"How much attention should I be paying? We're not in a hurry to get anywhere. I like driving around with you. I like being with you, period."

He smiled at that.

"So I'm just relaxing," she said. "I trust you to get us where we're going, wherever it is."

Up ahead, the light flashed green and the cars inched forward. Luke maneuvered around another pedestrian, an angry-looking woman who had stepped off the curb and close to the car as though daring someone to run over her foot.

"That woman has a death wish," he muttered.

"Or some really amazing self-confidence," Amelia said.

"She won't be feeling so confident when someone crushes her toes with a tire."

"Ouch."

Behind them, the woman darted between two standing cars and vanished.

Luke made a quick right-hand turn and the car cruised up a narrow side street.

"Okay, I'll bite. Where are we going?" Amelia said.

"I have to stop at home."

"Ooooh, so we're headed for the Upper East Side palace," she said. "Are your parents there?"

"I'm not sure," he said. He looked sidelong at her. "Got something in mind?"

She grinned. "Dunno."

He stroked her arm, deliberately trailing his fingers along the sensitive, blue-veined skin on her inner wrist. She felt her pulse quicken. His touch was exciting, almost unfamiliar—she tried, and failed, to recall the last time they'd slept together. Ten days, maybe twenty? In the final weeks of the semester, as she tried to prepare, pack, tie up each and every loose end, things had cooled between her and Luke. The love was still there, she thought, but circumstances were making things difficult. He was busy and frustrated, staying up late to study, coming out for parties or dinners only when she begged—and then, when he did, standing sullen and resentful in a corner.

He was consumed by the pressing responsibilities of the present. But she felt the future, with all of its untraveled roads and unexplored possibilities, unfurling slowly in front of her. She had even thought the unthinkable, *Maybe college relationships aren't meant to last,* but had always kissed him good night and then trudged back across campus to her own bed without asking to talk.

She could bide her time.

She was on the edge of a precipice, one that she could leap from at her leisure. She was free to go anywhere, to see Japan or Europe or even a cornfield in Iowa—if that was what she wanted.

Even now, sinking deep into the car seat and feeling the comfort, the safety and stability of his presence, she wasn't sure whether this trip together might be their last. But the feel of his fingertips, and the memory of nights spent in his arms, was making her breath come faster.

"You'd better watch the road," she warned.

"Okay," he sighed with mock-regret, "but when we get there, prepare to be ravaged."

In spite of herself, she giggled.

CHAPTER 9

The yard was a minefield of tossed trash: oil cans, car parts, cigarette butts, the carcasses of cars in differing states of decay. We picked our way around the mess. The front door of the house banged and boards groaned heavily as Craig stepped out on the porch.

"Jeeeeesus," I said, my voice floating out from clenched teeth.

James elbowed me.

"Stop that," he hissed.

"But look at him," I hissed back. "What happened?"

Craig had once had the kind of sturdy heft that made people think of football players, big calves and bracing shoulders and a leather-strap-snapping neck that supported a head just slightly too small for his body, a face with deep-set eyes that peered from beneath a heavy, furrowed forehead. Now, he was padded with pendulous flesh that seemed to pool around his ankles, choke his wrists, strangle and chafe at the bases of his fat fingers. As he waddled across the porch and saluted us, he just looked like a . . .

"Giant baby," I muttered. "Holy shit, he's a two-ton infant."

James snorted violently but shot me another, angrier warning look.

"Hey, man," Craig called. I hung back, feeling nervous. He looked at me and shifted uncomfortably. "Hey."

He squinted at me, opened his mouth as though he meant to say something else, then changed his mind and looked back at James. "Everyone's out in the yard."

We tripped gingerly up the creaky porch steps and walked through the house. One step over the threshold revealed a wrecked place: stuffing erupted from the upholstered sofa; strips of flypaper thick with the bodies of bluebottles hung from the ceiling; the smell of garbage floated just beneath the cheap sugary odor of a vanilla-scented air freshener.

"What have you been doing up here for the past week? This place looks like shit," said James, warily but not without affection.

"Supposedly, I'm 'packing up the house,'" said Craig grinning. "Someone had to clean out all the old-lady crap after Grammy Mitchell croaked, right? So I flew out, and I settled in, and I've been waking up drunk since last Tuesday."

I looked around the room, a landscape littered with

Chinese takeout containers and pizza boxes and empty beer cans that teetered on windowsills or nestled in the cushions of the couch.

"And never going to bed hungry, apparently," I said. James shot me another look.

"I mean, which is AWESOME!" I added, shooting one back and forcing a smile that I hoped looked enthused.

Craig fixed me with narrow eyes, then relaxed and grinned.

"Yes, yes it is," he said.

"What about your parents?" asked James.

Craig's smile disappeared.

"You know they won't come within five hunded miles of this place if they can help it."

Nobody replied and he looked suddenly, fleetingly uncomfortable—staring at the floor, rubbing the toe of a grubby sneaker against a caked-on reddish splotch that might have been pizza sauce and that flaked away from the linoleum.

A breeze blew through the house, banging the screen door lightly and carrying the scent of charcoal and meat to where we stood. My stomach kicked once and then settled. I swallowed. My tongue felt thick.

"Grill's on," Craig said, perking up and clapping James on the shoulder. "Come on."

He turned, avoiding looking at me, and clomped down the hall toward the back of the house. James offered a beckoning finger and followed, moving lightly in the shadow of Craig's enormous girth.

In another life, another time, another town, it wouldn't have been like this. Craig would have been too cruel, and James too smart, for their coincidental friendship to have ever lasted so long. But here, where James felt so trapped, Craig was exotic. Interesting. Something different, half outside and half in. Bridgeton blood, but a big-city dressing. He straddled the line between here and there, showing up each summer in the last weeks of school, disappearing again in the last days of August. He was living proof of a life lived elsewhere; there had even been a time, before I knew him better, when I'd thought we might be friends.

Richard Mitchell, like any small-town smart kid, had moved on and made good, never looking back. College in another state; a life on another coast; an aging mother whom he never came home to see but who couldn't be prouder of her absent boy.

"My Ricky," is what Bea Mitchell would say—clicking her dentures, so pleased and proud, hands together and with her white-whale bingo arms sagging against her housedress. "Did I tell you, my Ricky is in California?"

To me, Ricky was only a ghost. An urban legend, a face in a yearbook, a guy who had left and never come back. But his son was real enough—sent back to stay with Grandma by his parents at age twelve, and for every summer thereafter, when it became obvious that he was what guidance counselors and kiddie shrinks tactfully referred to as "difficult." Smart, manipulative, a little too good at lying, and a little too given to "accidentally" harming his younger sister. During the year, he could be kept safely away—turned over to more capable hands, closely watched from September to May by the staff at expensive boarding schools.

But there was still the summer to contend with, and it was a good idea, they all agreed, to remove him to a place with fewer opportunities for trouble—a bomb dropped in the remotest possible location, with the hopes that all the surrounding nothingness would damper its effects. And while the previous generation's namesake had fled for bigger things, his son had been drawn back in—straddling the line between outside and inside, finding a sense of home here in the town that his father had turned his back on. It wasn't hard to see what drew Craig to Bridgeton. Despite his outsider upbringing, the powerful otherness conferred by his California birth certificate, they had so much in common. My earliest memory of him was at someone's birthday party in the weeks just after ninth grade; he'd been sitting on a patch of grass, surrounded by a pack of kids in thrall to his summertime strangeness, pulling the legs off a beetle with methodical focus.

Even with every opportunity, even with a big house to play in and a faraway city to call home, Craig's favorite pastime had always been to destroy things.

We emerged through the back door onto a haphazard patio. A couple kids were sprawled on lawn chairs, the rest piled onto a stained couch that looked as though it had been left outside all winter.

"Rebecca!" A shrieking girl disentangled herself from the couch pile, spilling her beer, and launched herself at me.

"Lindsay," I said, catching her as she tripped over the leg of a patio chair. She grinned and breathed yeasty air into my face.

"Heeey," she said, "watch out for my tits!"

Lindsay had been gifted with enormous breasts on an otherwise average-size body, and it was a constant topic of conversation—because Lindsay liked it that way. She'd been thrilled when someone nicknamed her "Titsy," and signed everyone's yearbook with a P.S. that read, *Don't forget to come back and visit me and my two girls!*

I helped Lindsay regain her footing. "Do you and your tits need another drink?"

"Ha-ha! Come sit!" she chirped, taking my hand. I settled next to her, waving at everyone else. Jenna Kent, who had been in my English class and whose hair was now platinum blond after having grown steadily lighter throughout the year, gestured at a grimy-looking cooler.

"Beer?"

"Sure."

I took it, sipped, and tried to ignore the lurch in my stomach, and looked toward the grill. James and Craig stood next to it, deep in conversation. Craig frowned at whatever James was saying and poked at a slowly blackening hot dog with a pair of tongs.

"Hey, Rebecca, where've you been?" Lindsay asked, leaning forward to maximize the view of her cleavage.

Getting my heart broken, I thought. *Watching my parents not talk to each other.*

"Nowhere."

By midnight, the lengthening shadows in the yard had become pitch-black and impenetrable. James was on the couch with me now. He had put his arm around me in spite of the heat. Everyone was drunk. The conversation was noticeably quieter—partly because Lindsay was gone, had slipped away with Craig somewhere beyond the halo cast by the back-porch light. And partly because the subject was murder.

Jeff Francis, brother of Jack, privy to overheard conversations about the police investigation into the girl's death, was holding court.

"You know how there was all that blood in the road?" he had said, and sat back with a satisfied smile. "It all came out of her head. Her skull was, like, totally crushed on one side."

"Ew," someone said.

Jenna's eyes glittered. "Is that how she died?"

Jack nodded and looked into the distance, and the smile drooped at the corners. He swallowed hard. I wondered whether his inside information included things that weren't so much tantalizing as *terrible* . . . things he wished he didn't know.

"Jeff?"

He sighed.

"Probably. They won't know until the autopsy is done.

But, I mean, she was beaten to hell, you guys. Broken bones everywhere . . ." He took a long swig of beer, then sat back and muttered, "You know what? I shouldn't be talking about this."

Jenna looked exasperated, and Jeff refused to meet anyone's eyes. James cut in.

"Well, it's all speculation anyway," he said. "No point in talking about it, right? If they knew what happened, someone would have said something by now."

Hot, sweating, and feeling the buzz of my second beer, I looked pointedly at him. "They're gonna have a hard time knowing what happened, as long as people keep getting in the wa—"

James shot me a furious look, but I never finished; the close, hot space of the backyard was suddenly filled with the reverberating squall of Lindsay's high-pitched scream.

I whirled and looked toward the door. James leaped to his feet, brandishing an empty bottle by the neck. There was another scream, a series of thumps, and then she burst from the house. She'd lost her shirt somewhere; her "girls" flailed meatily inside a polka dot–patterned bra as she cleared the porch stairs in a single leap. The door banged hard behind her, shaking the house and unleashing a cascade of grit from the gutters.

"What the hell is wrong with you?" Jenna demanded, also jumping to her feet.

Lindsay looked around at us, wild-eyed, then crossed her arms over her chest and turned back toward the house.

Her mouth opened and closed once. We stared at her.

The door banged again. Craig stood on the steps in nothing but a pair of boxers, his face wrinkled in an expression that looked like a cross between misery and disgust.

He was holding a grease-stained Chinese food box in his hands.

"Oh my God!" Lindsay screamed. "Get it away!"

Craig grimaced and then snapped, "Would you shut up? You're not fucking helping!"

Jeff stood up from the couch, swayed a little, sat back down. "What's going on?"

"Oh my God, you guys," Lindsay said urgently. Everyone stared.

The Chinese food box was full, very full, of noodles.

They were moving.

James stepped forward, peering at the box, and addressed Craig. "Dude, what's in there?"

Craig looked at the ground and muttered something unintelligible.

"What?" said James.

"I said, 'worms,'" said Craig.

Lindsay shrieked again. Craig gave James a long-suffering look, then turned to her and said, "Seriously. Shut up."

Walking to the garbage cans that lined the patio, he kicked the top off one and dropped the box onto the brimming heap of trash. Even in the low light, the contents could be seen writhing around inside. There was a chorus of disgusted sounds from the gathered group.

"Dude," said Jeff.

Craig turned on unsteady feet and sat heavily on one of the patio chairs, looking dazed.

"Hey, man, maybe you should get dressed," James said, making an ambiguous gesture toward the porch door. Craig looked at him, looked down at the ample rolls of his gut, and then disappeared into the house.

The door slammed. All eyes fixed immediately on Lindsay.

"Oh my God," she said, and sat heavily on the couch. "That shit was sitting on the arm of the sofa; he went to take his shirt off and knocked it onto my *arm*."

People began to giggle. Lindsay glared at us and opened another beer, wrapping her lips around the top and sucking with exaggerated vigor. The door to the house banged open and Craig emerged, pulling a shirt over his head and grunting back down the porch steps.

"You didn't have to scream like that," he said to her.

"Oh, really?" she replied, sitting forward and sneering at him. "I'll remember that the next time I *cover you in worms*."

Jenna leaned against the house with her arms folded, watching mosquitoes get fried one by one in the electric-blue light of the bug zapper. Lindsay looked up at her.

"What's going on here, did I miss something?"

"Not really. We were talking about the news," Jenna said. "You know, the dead girl."

"Yeah?"

Jenna's voice was cold. "Not much to report, apparently."

Lindsay shuddered.

"I don't like thinking about that. I mean, geez, she got killed, like, right there." She pointed in the direction of the woods, where the thick-growing trees gave way to a steep hillside, and below it, the curve of Route 128. As if on cue, the muted *whoosh* of a passing car drifted through the night air. Gooseflesh broke out on my arms and legs as I realized that if the girl had screamed, had called out, had made any sound at all, it would be heard up here. Craig, dozing drunk on the sagging couch, celebrating his bare scrape through high school with a D+ average, would have opened his eyes to the sound of death creeping softly through the trees.

Jenna had realized it, too.

"Craig," she said.

He looked at her.

She leaned toward him. "You were here that night, weren't you?"

He met her eyes for a moment, then shrugged and stared into the distance.

"Dunno," he said.

Jenna looked exasperated. "You don't know? Are you kidding?"

"Hey, lay off," he snapped. "What do you care, huh? Why should I tell you where I was?"

She sat back and glared icily at him.

"Because," she said, "that girl practically died in your backyard. So if you were here, you would have heard something. And if you weren't here, then I wonder where you *did* go—" She looked at Lindsay now, who was beginning to look upset—"and with who."

Jenna swayed on her feet, just a little, and with a rush of understanding I realized that she was drunk. Her irritation was irrational, paranoid, illogical but growing anyway as Craig refused to give her what she wanted. Craig glowered back. Three more mosquitoes floated eerily toward the blue light of the bug zapper and incinerated themselves against the electric glow.

And then, meeting her eyes, Craig smiled.

"It's none of your business. And even if I was here," he said, and Lindsay's mouth opened slightly as though she was going to speak, but he stood up and pushed a meaty finger into Jenna's face. "Even if I *was*, it wouldn't matter, because I wouldn't give a shit about that dead bitch if she'd crawled into my yard and died on the doorstep."

The patio had cleared, then—Jenna making a disgusted sound and exiting with an, "I'm gone," Lindsay demanding to know why Craig had to be such an asshole all the time before following. Jeff, who had been standing at the fringes of the group and watching the exchange with wide eyes, muttered something about being their designated driver and shuffled after them.

With the sound of Jeff's car fading in the distance, Craig sat down on the couch with a fresh beer in hand. His fat face was swollen with proud ignorance, smug self-satisfaction. James could say what he wanted, but it couldn't be clearer: Craig was intentionally getting in the way of the investigation. He liked the idea of the dead girl—"that dead bitch"—remaining a no-name corpse, unclaimed and unsolved.

"You should have let the police do their job."

Craig looked at James. James jerked his head in my direction and said, "Word's going around."

Craig shrugged, a strange little smile playing at the corners of his mouth. "Hey, I don't make the laws. Law says they need a warrant, they need a warrant."

"Or you can give permission, you dickhead," I snapped. "Instead of making things difficult." I looked at James for help. He shook his head and mouthed, *Stop.* I stared at him.

"What?" he asked, staring back.

"Aren't you going to say anything? I'm sorry, but what if her killer *was* out there? What if he dropped something, evidence or something, that could've helped them, but they didn't find it because Craig is an asshole?"

Craig was watching the exchange with that same, weird smile.

"Well, they're definitely not gonna find it now," he said. "Even when they do get a judge's say-so."

The words hung in the air as James turned to look at him.

"What are you talking about?"

Craig shrugged. "Let's just say that I did a little cleanup in the yard today. Let's just say that if there was something to find, it's gone now."

I gaped. Even someone like Craig, someone who'd always taken a little too much pleasure in other people's suffering, wouldn't take evidence from a crime scene. Would he? It had to be a joke.

"Bullshit."

"Try again."

James's voice floated out of the darkness; he'd moved away from us without my seeing.

"Did you really find something?" he asked.

"I found lots of things," Craig grinned. "And if one of them was important, well, I guess that'll just be too bad."

"Are you kidding? If you found something"—I was sputtering, my voice rising in pitch—"you have to give it to the police!"

Craig's smile kept stretching. "Fat chance. What do I care about some dead, beat-up bitch? And why should I help your incompetent redneck police do their job?"

There was a long silence.

"I'm going to tell them about this," I said, realizing as the words came out how pathetic I sounded, hating the plaintive whine in my voice.

"Like hell you will."

"Becca," said James. He had reappeared behind me without my noticing. He put a hand on my shoulder. "He's just kidding. Just trying to give you a hard time. Right?"

Craig didn't answer, but shrugged.

"CRAIG. Come on, man. Give it up."

The big hands went up in mock surrender.

"Yeah, yeah, okay? Sure. Just having some fun."

"Oh, so now it's all a big joke?" I snapped. "Is this funny to you? Maybe Craig doesn't care about catching a murderer, but—"

"Hey, *Rebecca*," Craig said, sneering my name like it was a dirty word, "if you care so much, why don't you go wait out by the side of the road for a while? Maybe he'll come back."

I stood up, ready to fight.

James stepped between us, his voice cutting through the tension. "Stop it. Both of you."

I looked at his face and realized how unsteady I felt on my feet. My head was heavy, clouded by the beer. I was tired of arguing.

"Fine," I said. I sat heavily on the couch. "Fine."

For a minute, no one spoke; there was only the incessant noise of the crickets, the hum of the bug zapper, the shorted-fuse sound the mosquitoes made as they incinerated themselves. My hair clung to my neck. It was so still, so hot.

James moved to sit beside me, stroking my arm.

"Let it go, all right?" he whispered. The hairs rose on the back of my neck as his breath touched them.

"All right," I sighed.

"We can go now. Do you want to go?"

"Yes."

Craig walked us back through the house ("Watch out for worms," said James.) and stood under the porch light as we picked our way through the yard. His features, lit from above, stood out in harsh relief.

The motor coughed and rattled as I slammed my door. The car began to roll. As we reached the end of the drive, I rolled my window open and peered over my shoulder to where Craig still stood on the porch. He wasn't watching us go; his eyes were aimed, unfocused, into the dark woods—and at the road beyond, where drifting, red-tinted dust still marked the place where a life had ended too soon. I shuddered as I watched him, then felt the tension rush out of my body as we turned the corner and started down the road.

But when I closed my eyes, I could still see him—standing there, staring into the dark.

Looking out at the place where the girl had died, and smiling.

AMELIA

"That was amazing."

Luke was looking down at her, propped up on one elbow and covered with a sheen of slick sweat, still breathing heavily. "Amazing," he said again.

Amelia pulled the sheet over her naked body, looked up at him and smiled, trying not to roll her eyes. Luke's so-called "ravaging" had started out promising—they had crashed through his bedroom door in a panting tangle, all grappling arms and flying clothing—but then, like always, it had wound up as ten uninspired minutes of banging in the missionary position. The headboard had tapped the wall so rhythmically that she could have set a watch by it. She had tried to make it interesting, whispering in his ear and clawing at his back, telling him what she wanted him to do to her. But Luke, who had been almost unrecognizable when he threw her onto the bed with exhilarating, animal intensity, had looked shocked, then shushed her and settled into the usual routine. He was back in his comfort zone. As she looked at him, she realized that he was still wearing his glasses . . . and his socks.

Ugh, she thought.

He was staring down at her, expecting a reply.

"Mmm," she said.

"Are you upset with me?"

She looked away. "Not exactly."

"Look, I'm sorry. I just get nervous when you . . . talk. It's weird. It's harsh; it sounds dirty."

"Sex is dirty," she said. "That's part of the fun, you know."

"Not when you're in love." He rolled out of the bed, pulled on his boxers, walked a few agitated paces across the floor. She watched him. He padded over to the dresser, opened a drawer, and began pulling out shirts, tossing them onto the foot of the bed.

"Do the two have to be mutually exclusive?" she said. The patient feeling had come back. "Sweet sex is nice, but it doesn't have to be like that every time. And it doesn't mean that I love you less."

He didn't answer, but closed the drawer—hard—and moved on to the one below it. A few pairs of socks and underwear joined the pile at the foot of the bed. He looked at her again, quickly, almost furtively. She sat up, letting the sheet fall into her lap, breasts exposed. Even though he'd seen them hundreds of times before, his face reddened and he turned away.

"Hey," she said. He pulled open the next drawer.

"I don't want to fight about this," he muttered.

"We're not fighting," she said. "We're just talking. I'm talking to you. Don't you ever want to fuck? Not make love, just, fuck?"

"I don't know."

Her voice was breathier. "No? Haven't you ever thought about grabbing me from behind and throwing me against the wall? Just taking what you wanted?" She stepped out of bed, crossed the room in three steps, the blond wood cold against her bare feet, and pushed her body against his. He whirled to face her and gripped her shoulders. His eyes narrowed. She slid her knee between his legs.

"Come on," she said, curling her fingers into the knots of hard muscle at his waist. "Come on."

She lifted her chin, defiant, raising her mouth closer to his. They stared at each other. And then, suddenly so that she barely had time to take a breath, he kissed her so hard that her ears popped.

CHAPTER 10

*I*t was hard to understand Stan Murray with his mouth full, but the subject matter was unmistakable.

"Crime of passion," he grunted, though the words came out sounding more like *Kind of puffin*. "Definitely. And not no stranger, either. She had a big fat handprint on her face, like someone got right up close and walloped her before she even saw it coming."

Lindsay sailed past me with a piece of cheesecake, casting a glance toward Stan's openmouthed gesturing and rolling her eyes. Her presence jolted me back to reality; I'd been lurking near the bar, eavesdropping and mind racing, listening for any hint that they might be closer to understanding how and why the beautiful, battered body of a stranger had come to rest just outside the town line.

"There's nothing grosser than that jackass trying to

talk around a burger," she said, oblivious to my focus, then disappeared into the dining room.

I was glad to have her there. Lindsay had started working just after the Fourth of July, her presence adding another beat to the busy rhythm of the place; the buzz of conversation and clinking of glassware undulated in time with the shuffling of summer people in and out of the wood-paneled dining room, until, like the tremulous high note of a showstopping aria, Lindsay's high-pitched voice would drift out of the kitchen and over to the bar.

She had a way with words.

"Fuck you, Kevin Kelly!" she screeched a moment later, barreling back toward the kitchen as the prissy man who ran the front of the house fled and the short-order cooks cackled behind their cupped hands. "Why don't you pour yourself another fucking martini, you alkie asshole!"

Kevin charged past me, blowing furious air from his too-large nostrils and muttering unintelligibly under his breath. He was an out-of-work actor with a receding hairline, an ego that seemed to leak from his ears, sweat-stained shirts that were too loose in the shoulders but strained across the stout paunch of his gut. He also had a drinking problem. At four thirty, the first person to arrive for the dinner shift would invariably find him perched at the end of the bar, guiltily sucking at the rim of a pint glass that was full of something we all called "water" and which we all knew was nothing of the sort.

I watched as he pounded his way into the staircase alcove where the waitstaff did sidework, ricocheted awkwardly off one wall, rattled the dishes stacked neatly in the tall built-in cupboard, and finally grabbed a baseball-size piece of bread from the ready basket and hurled it down the hallway.

In the kitchen, Lindsay was mock-curtsying while Tom chortled and applauded.

"What did you say?" I said, casting a cursory glance over my shoulder. Kevin had disappeared in the direction of the bar. "Kevin Kelly just got violent with a dinner roll."

"*Pffft,*" said Lindsay, and started giggling again.

"Hey, what the hell!" a voice said. We both looked sharply toward the oven, where Tom was standing with one indignant hand on his hip and twin beads of sweat inching slowly down his temples. "I baked those, goddamnit."

I struggled to think of something witty to say, but my mind only churned sluggishly in one place, dredging up bits of overheard conversation.

Beaten. Broken. Someone she knew.

Lindsay looked sidelong at me, tossed her hair, and giggled at Tom. "So what?"

"It's just not right, that's all," he said, then turned back to the oven.

"Yeah, okay, Tommy." Lindsay rolled her eyes, then grabbed my arm and dragged me through the kitchen to the small back door that opened onto the street.

Tom was still muttering as we slipped outside.

"It takes some nerve, is all. You oughta not mess with another man's rolls."

Lindsay clasped my hand and pulled me around the side of the building, into the garbage alley that ran the length of its rear. Back here, the only light was a high-mounted outdoor fixture that cast an orangey glow over the crumbling brick of the wall we stood beside, draping weak light over her shoulders like a sick sun. A nearby Dumpster was a shapeless mass of heavy black.

I was grateful for the dark. I had begun to hate the sight of people in the daytime: the way their eye sockets turned to brownish caves in the harsh, high sun; the way the shadows settled grotesquely in the furrows of their faces; the dimpled and gravelly fat that revealed itself in pockets on their thighs and triceps.

I hated the way their eyes seemed to pierce me, hated their endless questions about my plans, my plans.

I had tried again and again to see myself gone. I closed my eyes and turned my mind toward September—walking the long, paved paths that lined the quad; lounging in the hallways of a well-worn dormitory; laughing alongside dozens of fresh-faced kids, the new friends I hadn't yet met. I struggled to hear it: the clicking keys of students at work; the cacophony of a cafeteria with no shushing chaperones or watchful adults; the crunch of future feet over fallen leaves shot through with orange and ochre.

I couldn't hold it. It was the ghost of what would have been; it turned transparent and disintegrated as I watched. It turned to dust—sunbaked and tinged with blood, swirling so thick and hot that it blocked out tomorrow.

And when I was alone, a small, sneering voice inside my head would whisper, "Serves you right."

Because this was what happened to girls who make plans. The overconfident, the forward-looking, the ones who mapped their futures and filed them away, so sure that the world would embrace them. I had had mine forever—a five-year blueprint, a series of boxes to be checked, a recipe for escape that I drew up and then set aside, believing that it would simply stay just as I'd left it. That it was meant to happen just so. That the summer would slip blissfully by, and nothing would change, not until the very last moment, bittersweet but must-do, when I packed my life into the trunk of a car and left behind my high school sweetheart. Just as we'd always known I would. I knew just how it would go; I'd planned it out in theatrical detail, framing the scene with cinematic nuance. The words we would both say; the wistful smile that would play on James's lips; the tears that would fill my eyes and crack my voice, but never fall. The last rays of sun would light the space between us, glowing gold between our tilted faces while we kissed each other good-bye.

I knew just how he would look, growing smaller in my rearview, standing still and tall like a slender reed in the dying light.

That's how it was meant to end; we would kiss, and cry, and play our roles to perfection.

He was not supposed to pull my plans out from under me. My beautiful, brilliant blueprints were not supposed to be torn in two and cast aside. The summer was not supposed to start with something so brutally broken.

There was not supposed to be blood on the road.

That girl, dead and gone, her spirit trapped forever just inside town limits—she'd come from someplace, was going somewhere. Until destiny had stepped into the road in front of her, stopped her forward motion, drawn a killing claw across the white, fluttering swell of her future. Whispering, "Oh no, you don't."

When you made plans, the saboteurs came out to play.

A long, thin cigarette emerged from behind Lindsay's ear; she put a flame to the end. I watched her lips part and then come together again, wrapping wetly around the filter. She did this at parties, sucking with self-conscious gusto at the tip, allowing her cheeks to hollow with the effort and enjoying the captivated looks on the faces of nearby boys.

I was staring.

"What?" she said.

I blinked, then shook my head, leaning back against the cool brick and forcing a laugh. "Are you trying to seduce me?"

She laughed—genuine, unlike mine, unself-conscious and easy. She exhaled lazily, tilting her head back and watching as the smoke lifted in languid curls toward the rooftop. "Force of habit," she said, then shook her head and grinned again.

I rolled my head against the wall. The brick barely

touched the side of my cheek. It was like cold sandpaper, a rough caress. I thought of James, and my breath caught in my throat.

"You okay?" Lindsay asked.

"Yeah. Fine."

"You looked pretty out of it back there," she said, gesturing back toward the restaurant. "That stuff bothers you, huh? It's pretty gross, right? I don't think Stan's even supposed to be talking about it."

"It doesn't bother me, really," I said. "I just was hoping . . . I don't know." I trailed off, then felt my body stiffen as Lindsay suddenly shifted her weight next to me. She had moved next to me, leaning against the wall, when she suddenly laid her head on my shoulder.

"Rebecca Williams," she cooed at me. "Are you actually getting *interested* in the local goings-on?"

I struggled to laugh; it was meant to be a joke. She had no way of knowing that all summer long, late at night, I'd lain awake and felt myself dragged down by questions— echoes of townie chatter that circled the dusty roadside and pelted the corpse who lay still in a cold, stainless-steel drawer and kept her bloodless blue-gray lips closed tight against the onslaught.

Who are you?

Who killed you?

Where is he now?

There were no answers, and the investigation was slowing. Information trickled out now in dribs and drabs, yielding nothing significant, but it didn't matter. We hungered for it.

I hungered for it.

The last-year-me wouldn't have. That girl, forward-looking and future-focused, wasn't interested in what happened here. It was *there* that I wanted, out there somewhere, when I sat elbow-to-elbow with my giggling friends and let my thoughts swirl up and away from the three-mile radius of our small lives. In my head, I careened out of town and across state lines, until the landscape became strange and unfamiliar. I wanted to see all of it. Everything. The vast expanses of the flat Midwest, miles of horizontal earth with the curving horizon at its end. Strange, stunted trees and driftwood skeletons on the lonely windswept beaches of the farthest coasts. Towering oaks hung thick with the gray lace of Spanish moss, looming like hovering parents over shaded southern dirt. The California sun, dipping and disappearing into the ocean, tipping the waves with orange light.

The yearning for elsewhere had always left me only half engaged with the day-to-day of here. I was aloof, strange, disinterested in the little whirlings of our high school world. Some people thought it made me suspicious, untrustworthy. Even Craig, who knew firsthand the existence of Somewhere Else, thought I was dreaming beyond my rights.

"For small-town trash," he'd said to me a few days after our first meeting, "you think awfully highly of yourself."

Lindsay was still peering at me, curious.

"Me, interested. Yeah, that would be weird, right?" I joked, and reached a hand up to pat Lindsay's cheek. She giggled back, in character, always ready to play the flirt. I wondered how it was that this impersonal warmth, the maneuvering sweetness of a girl I'd grown up alongside without ever really knowing, could make me feel better. Lighter. My fingers uncurled and lay slack and comfortable at my side; I hadn't known I was clenching them.

"Out of character, more like it," she laughed. "But you know, I totally understand." She lifted her head and looked at me, her eyes like black pools in the opaque orange light.

"Oh, yeah?" I said, and instantly felt sorry for it. The words had come out fast and too bitter.

"I just mean, I think I get how you feel," she said. She held her hands up, palms facing forward, a living illustration of *Hey, man, didn't mean nothing.* "You're gone at the end of the summer, right? If I were going away to school, I wouldn't care about any of this small-town bullshit either."

"You're not going to school?" I feigned the surprise I wished I felt. It happened every year—kids who graduated like all the rest, but seemed to cast roots into the ground the moment they left the stage and the final strains of "Pomp and Circumstance" had faded. They retreated toward the center of town, wrapped themselves in the familiar fabric of life in Bridgeton, gossiped and grew fat on a steady diet of sameness. Eventually, they would marry another lingerer and give birth to children who, more likely than not, would also grow up to stay put.

"Community college, maybe?" she said. "It's just . . . you know, it's expensive. And I don't even know what I'd get out of it."

"It's different for everyone, I guess," I said quietly. Inside, I stretched my imagination again, trying to see myself in a new life at State and encountering nothing but thick, featureless fog.

"So I'm going to hang out here," she continued. "Wait tables, save some money, decide what to do. Maybe I'll go away one day, go to school, or travel, or get a job-job. But I'm not above just being here a while."

"Hey, I'm not—"

Her eyes widened and she rushed in, "Oh no, I didn't mean it that way! I know you're not. It's not like I think you're some high-and-mighty bitch or anything. I mean, you've got this whole life planned out, you know? Me, I don't know what I want to be, or do, or anything."

The swirling bugs that fluttered and flew against the orange alley light had finally noticed that there was fresh meat below. A mosquito floated past Lindsay's head, whined beneath my chin, and settled on my chest, where it plunged its sucker into a fleshy spot just above my left breast. I watched it, counted to three, then brought my hand down savagely against my own skin. The bug disappeared in a mash of legs, wings, my own blood.

"Believe it or not," I said, quietly, "I think I know how you feel."

CHAPTER 11

I woke just before noon to the sunlight that came streaming through our house's south windows and filled every room with choking brightness. It bathed the walls, warmed the faded rugs, shattered against the dangling prisms that my mother had hung in every window. My bedroom was full of rainbows that swept smoothly over the walls. Back and forth, slipping lightly along the surface of my bedside table with its framed photos and green glass lamp.

There was a light knock, and the door creaked open.

"Honey? I think you should wake up, now."

I rolled over to see my mother, dressed for gardening. A pair of rough gloves was stuffed into her pants' pocket and her face was marked with thin smears of dirt, but her hands and fingernails were pink and clean.

She moved into the room, stopping by my desk and patting the thick pile of papers that sat there.

"You know, your packing list for college came. It's over here. You've seen it, right?"

"No," I said. It was only half a lie. The fat packet of orientation materials had been sitting in the same place since it arrived, when I rifled through the thick sheaf of papers and glossy brochures that smelled like glue, but couldn't bring myself to read them.

"We could go over it together," my mother said. She settled next to me on the bed and reached a hand out to stroke my hair.

"Maybe later," I said. "I'm supposed to . . . see James."

A real lie; the night before, James had dropped me at my door along with the news that he would be missing until next week. I imagined that they'd already begun the day's brutal task, him and his father, sitting in the dark and dust of a long-shuttered room and gently sifting the contents of its drawers, desks, and closets. They were starting to go through his mother's things.

"How are things going, there?"

"What do you mean?" I struggled to sit up, leaning back against the headboard. It creaked under my weight.

"You and James," she said.

I shrugged. "Fine."

"Fine?" She gave me a pointed look.

"Mom, I just woke up. The whole subtlety thing isn't really happening for me right now."

"Okay, okay," she said, holding her hands up in surrender. "What I mean is, your father and I are . . . concerned."

My breath caught in my throat.

"About me?"

She knew. Everyone else was looking through me, but she could see me struggling.

"No, honey," she said, and then smiled at me with so much clueless confidence that I wanted to scream and fling myself against the wall. "We know we don't have to worry about you. But for James, your leaving is bound to be hard. You helped him through a rough time."

Inside, I had gone flat and cold.

"Mom, I'll handle it."

"I know," she said. "But I hope you'll do the right thing. You don't want him to assume . . ."

My temper flared. "Would you stop acting like James is some kind of helpless puppy? You have no idea what's happening with us, okay? I mean, it's not like he's never done anything—" I was going to say *wrong*, but my mother cut me off.

"I'm not criticizing him!" she exclaimed. "I'm sure he's got plenty going on. And of course I think he's a very nice boy, and he obviously cares a great deal for you. I just worry, honey, because soon you'll be on divergent paths."

"Jesus, Mother—"

She held up a hand again. "I know, you know that. I know. But I'm your mother, and as long as you're still under my roof, it's my job to give you guidance when I think you need it. And right now, and I'm not saying this is your fault, but James clearly isn't thinking about what will happen when you leave. And that will end up hurting him. It will."

I stared at her, wanting to laugh at how much she

didn't get it, wanting to shout that for all his niceness and obvious caring, James had also bruised me and broken me in a way that drained all the color from my world. That I was derailed and drowning.

She mistook the look on my face for disbelief. The hand, the maternal hand of comfort, extended toward my leg and gave it a reassuring squeeze through the blankets.

"And the one thing I just wouldn't want—your father and I, we wouldn't want—to see you limiting yourself. Keeping up a long-distance relationship is already hard, but when one person's ambitions are so different from the other's . . . you're just in different places," she said, nodding in agreement with herself.

I sighed, watching the rainbows hurtling along the walls of the too-bright room, looking at the lines that had etched themselves into the skin near my mother's eyes and mouth, thinking of James, who would never even know the luxury of maternal disapproval.

"He doesn't have to stay here, you know," I said. "He's smart. He could go to college."

"I'm sure he could," she said. "But you need to worry about *you*."

"Mm-hmm."

"Becca, look at me."

I did.

My mother's face was a mask of concern as she said, "You need to start thinking about your future. James can take care of himself, and he's going to have to, because you have bigger fish to try. All you can do is be honest with him, and

I think that means you've got to be honest with yourself—"

"Mom—"

"—and remember that there's a great big world out there, waiting for you!"

Her words seemed to wrap around my throat.

The world began to spin.

When I made it to the bathroom, I threw up in the sink.

Once upon a time, the great big world outside Bridgeton had seemed like Xanadu—miles of golden road lined with smiling people, waiting to usher me through hundreds of open doors. There was nothing out there but bright light and possibilities. There were big dreams of other places, other people, even other boys.

There had even, for two hours in April, been somebody else.

He was a glimpse of the future, where I would live and breathe and love far, far away from this place. A future where behind a closed door, on Saturday mornings, a boy I hadn't yet met would wrap an arm around my waist and exhale damp heat into the curve of my neck. Where we would keep our eyes closed, pull the covers closer, burrow down deeper to escape the nine-o'clock sunshine, and the sound of heavy breath echoing along the rusted steel confines of a pickup truck would be nothing but a memory.

"Are you sure I shouldn't come with you?" James had said as he watched me try again to zip my backpack closed. I had overpacked, but each time I pulled my clothes back out and took stock of what I was bringing, it all seemed essential. I didn't want to be too cold, too hot, too casual, too high school. I didn't want to look like a visitor.

I kept my eyes down and busied myself with the zipper. "You don't have a place to stay."

He shrugged.

"And anyway," I added, "you'd be bored. I'm going to be busy getting orientated with the other pre-froshes."

He shrugged again. "It's just a day. I can find something to do. We could make a road trip out of it."

I crushed the bag between my knees and wrenched the zipper shut over the woolly bulge of a sweater, thinking as the teeth closed that I shouldn't have packed it. It was bulky and unsophisticated. It was everything I didn't want my future self to be.

James was looking at the floor, chewing on his lip. The casual feel of the conversation—the no-big-deal way that he'd tossed out the idea of coming along, as though it were just another nothing suggestion—was starting to erode. I realized as I looked at him that things had been like that a lot lately. Our summer romance had lasted so well, deepening as the seasons changed, staying bright and strong through the worst of winter. But between the easy familiarity of us, the inside jokes, the quiet comfort of watching him from the passenger side, was the shadow of summer and the *tick-tick-tick* of our time together drawing to a close.

Lately, I thought, James was having trouble ignoring the sound of the countdown. Lately, our conversations felt loaded, layered, imbued with double and triple meanings.

"This is something I need to do by myself."

"Need, or want?"

"Does it matter?"

When I kissed him good-bye through my car window, he joked, "I feel like I'm never going to see you again."

When I crossed the state line at eighty miles per hour, I thought, *You might not*.

It was March, and Bridgeton had been edging damply into spring; the air had turned soft and humid and carried the smell of thawing earth, and the lake had begun to swell with the melting snow. But two hundred miles north, I crossed back into winter again. The air was a slap in the face, bitter and biting, and the campus was a mess of mud punctuated by crusts of gritty, refrozen slush. Inside the admissions office, steam heat had fogged the windows.

There were a hundred of us, give or take. Seventeen and eighteen, all trying to look unself-conscious and cool despite the peel-and-stick name tags and overstuffed backpacks that gave us away as weekend interlopers. They herded us into a room, handed us folders that were emblazoned with the university crest and stuffed inside with campus maps, meal tickets, and a list titled "Things To Do" that conspicuously avoided any mention of alcohol. Over sandwiches and sodas, we exchanged information: names, states, intended majors. We were mostly from New England, except for one—a tanned, fit boy with wire-rimmed glasses who had flown up from Tallahassee, and who laughingly told us that he was planning to spend the winter months crying in the fetal position. I snorted too loudly, and next to me, a pink-cheeked blonde with a Coach bag looked sidelong at my shoes and said, "Where are you from?"

"Bridgeton," I said.

She blinked at me.

"You know, where Silver Lake is?" I asked.

"Oh," she said, picking the lettuce out of her wrap with long, manicured fingers. "I didn't know people actually lived there."

When she stood and left, joining the other kids who were drifting out with student hosts or going to audit a two o'clock class, Tallahassee looked after her and rolled his eyes.

"That was rude," he said.

"It happens," I said.

"If it makes you feel any better, my grandma would've called that girl a 'peroxide-loving whore,'" he said, grinning.

At the front of the room, more hosting students had appeared in a clump. An obese young woman, her cheeks chapped red from the cold, scanned the remaining crowd and then called out, "Rebecca Williams?"

"That's me," I said, hoisting my backpack. The fat girl—whose name turned out to be, hilariously, Bonnie Biggs—smiled and waved at me.

As I turned away, Tallahassee raised his hand in a half salute.

"See you later, Rebecca."

Even then, I didn't expect to. Even now, when I think back on that night, I come away knowing that it was pure chance: a gift from the universe, or maybe a test. When

I stepped out of Bonnie's room and padded down the cold stairs in search of a vending machine, it wasn't because I was looking to cheat.

I wasn't looking for anything. I had found what I was looking for. I'd sat in on an archaeology class that made me go cross-eyed with all the things I didn't know; I'd sat, exhilarated, in a cafeteria full of the shouts and laughter of a thousand kids just like me; that night, Bonnie had gamely taken me to a real, live party where the music was deafening and the floor was sticky with spilled beer and kids laughed and spun boozily into one another's arms. It was a perfect day, a twenty-four-hour trip into my own future that left me breathless with the magnitude of what lay ahead.

But when I tripped barefoot into the dorm's lounge that night, I found him there. He was propped on a threadbare couch, surrounded by four tired-looking kids who were passing a flask back and forth. As I stepped into the room, I heard somebody slur the words, "David Foster Wallace."

"Rebecca," he said, looking at me with heavy-lidded eyes.

"Tallahassee," I said.

"Are you looking for me?" he asked, grinning in a slushy way that made me think of bonfires, beer, and small-town summertime. Drunkenness: the great equalizer.

"I was looking for Gatorade, actually," I replied, causing the literary couch kids to explode with laughter. Tallahassee laughed, too—a sound so light and easy that it made me think suddenly of James, who was neither—and patted the empty spot next to him.

Of course, he wasn't Tallahassee. Of course he had a

name, but I don't remember it. It was gone by morning, had leached out of my brain overnight along with the content of our conversation, the books he'd recommended, the things we'd used to fill the time while we waited to be alone. We'd talked, an unspoken agreement passing between us, until the last lolling drinker had stumbled off to bed. He was getting nervous, I could tell; he'd started to fumble with his glasses, taking them off and then putting them on again, until the lenses were smudged and cloudy.

At some point, he'd told me his name.

But it didn't matter. It wasn't about this guy, who he was, the way he smiled, the taste of his mouth. He could have been anyone. He was an experiment. A test. A one-kiss chance to remember where I was going and what lay ahead. And he was something else, too: proof that in spite of how things had changed since that first night by the fire, I had not lost sight of my goal. That no matter what, I was not too in love with James to leave him behind.

That at four o'clock in the morning, when a smart Southerner with a winter tan passed me a flask, touched my cheek, and told me I was beautiful, I would not be afraid.

His breath smelled like warm whiskey, and when he kissed me, he wove his fingers into my hair.

That was before a pretty, bloodless body on the side of the road—a blue-lipped omen in a cotton dress—showed me just how much there was to be afraid of. Out there, in houses and cars and hidden in the shadows, were dark and unsmiling things with hard fists and sharp teeth.

I knew better now.

My mother appeared over my shoulder, pressing the cool damp of a towel to my temple.

"In the sink, huh?" she said. "That's classy."

"I'm sorry."

She chuckled. "Just aim for the toilet next time, okay?"

I gave her a thumbs-up and a weak smile.

"And, sweetie, I know this is tough, but you have to believe me: it's all going to be fine. These things have a way of working themselves out."

I nodded, and she left.

I wished I could believe her.

Because when James had kissed me last night, in the shadowed safety of the backyard, I had suddenly recalled the taste of Tallahassee's mouth—a secret left unsaid and pushed away, one I hadn't even thought of since the day that I came back and didn't tell.

This time, it came with the overwhelming urge to vomit.

My plans had faded and crumbled, the way dreams do when you open your eyes and realize in the bright light of day that none of it was real, that none of it was even possible. My old self made me sick, and I was grateful for the cover of darkness over my guilty face. It wasn't until James spoke, his voice vacant and hollow, that I realized he'd never have noticed. That he was miles away, calling back to me from a deep, dark hole made out of memory.

That, like me, he was thinking about someone else.

"Do you remember Brendan Brooks?" he'd asked, gazing into the distance.

My memory filled with a rush of glass-green water, bloodless hands, and open eyes, the ghost-pale boy body that lived eternally on the sinewy cusp of fifteen. James stared into space, cigarette dangling by his side, his pressed-tight lips not quite covering the sound of his grinding teeth.

"Of course, I do," I said. "Why?"

I reached out to touch the thin cloth of his T-shirt, trailing the backs of my fingers over the hard muscle of his arm. "Why?" I said again. "What made you think of him?"

James shook his head and looked at me. Through me. His eyes were shadowed holes in his drawn face, and when he spoke, it was to the air that lay on my shoulder.

"Not him," he said. "I've been thinking about his mother."

And then he had gone. Dry lips brushed my temple; I smelled sweet smoke and old leather as he kissed me and turned away. The car door had slammed before I could speak. The taillights grew faint in the distance, then disappeared.

He didn't look back.

AMELIA

Minutes later, breathing hard and with raw, red spots newly sprouted on her knees and elbows, she peered back and smiled. Luke was kneeling behind her. One of his hands still clutched her hip, the other was reaching up to straighten his glasses. He looked dazed.

"Now that," she said, "was amazing."

Luke mumbled something into his palm.

"What?"

"I said, 'Holy shit,'" he replied.

She laughed. He pulled away, grimacing a little, and sat back on his heels.

"I think I need a nap. Or at least a shower."

Amelia picked herself up from the floor and scouted the room for her underwear, finally pulling them from under the bed. She stepped into them gingerly, then faced the mirror. Most of her hair had found its way into a tangled mass at the back of her head, except for a few renegade bits that were sticking straight into the air.

"You need a shower; I need a hairbrush," she said. He stood up, teetered off balance for a minute, then leaned in to kiss her. His lips were sticky. She kissed him back, then licked the tip of his nose.

"Yuck," he said, laughing. "Hang on, I'll get you one." He cast a glance toward the floor, looking for his clothes, then shrugged and strode out of the room naked.

She gathered her dress from the floor and pulled it over her head, trying to smooth some of the wrinkles in the cotton, then surveyed her reflection again.

The girl who stared back at her, in spite of her wild appearance, skinned elbows, and the red splotches that bloomed on her chest, looked good, confident. She lifted her chin and appraised herself—wide-set eyes, thin lips, straight nose, blond hair that had shaped itself into a near-bouffant from all that rolling around between the sheets—then turned to take in the room.

It was undeniably Luke's room. She couldn't say for sure, not having known him before college, but she suspected that everything was just as he'd left it the day that he packed his things and soldiered off to school. It was the space of an aspiring adult—all muted tones and black wood furniture, the kind that would be featured in a catalog with a name like "The Executive Suite." The only sign of adolescent life was the poster that hung above his desk: a photograph of a blonde in a bikini, her lips pursed in a come-hither pout, one hand resting suggestively on her inner thigh. She had huge, fake breasts that seemed to float on her rib cage instead of being attached to it in any meaningful way.

Amelia rolled her eyes at the image. It wasn't the picture that bothered her, exactly, more that Luke's tastes could be so utterly . . .

Pedestrian, she thought. *Pamela-freakin-Anderson, cardboard cutout dull.*

"You're thinking that I'm totally unoriginal, aren't you," said Luke's voice behind her.

She turned, guilty but delighted that he'd somehow read her thoughts, and smiled at him. He was in the doorway, with a towel wrapped high around his waist like an old boxer.

"It was a present from my dad," he said. The promised hairbrush was in his hand, too, and he passed it to her as he looked ruefully up at the sex kitten on the wall.

"Interesting present," she said.

"I think he did it in lieu of having the 'birds and the bees' conversation with me," he said, shaking his head and laughing at the memory. "He couldn't bring himself to talk about sex, so my mom took over, and he just got me this poster. Like, 'Here, son. When you jerk off, this is what you should be thinking about.'"

"Thanks, Dad." She giggled.

"I should probably take it down."

"Wouldn't that hurt your father's feelings?"

"Well, I could give it back to him. Say, 'Hey, Dad, thanks for the masturbation material, but now I've got the real thing.'" He winked at her.

"Leave me out of it!" she laughed, cuffing him lightly on the ear. He caught her by the wrist and kissed her. She kissed him back. She kept her eyes open, watching him. How lovely it is, she thought, that someone so familiar can still surprise you.

He broke the kiss, moving his lips along her face and then planting a final smack on her neck.

"About that shower," he said. "Do you want to take one?"

She smiled up at him and shook her head, brandishing the hairbrush.

"All right, I'll just be ten minutes." He opened the door that led to the adjacent bathroom and looked back at her. "Do you need to get in here, for anything? I always forget to ask."

She shook her head again.

"I've never had to share a bathroom," he said, smiling. "Guess I'll have to get used to that before we move in together."

He disappeared behind the door.

He didn't notice that Amelia was standing frozen, the brush still raised in one hand, her mouth slightly open. Sighing, she turned to the mirror and brushed her hair, berating herself for not speaking up. She had been so close, the words were ready to come out—Luke, about that— but she'd shut her mouth on them. It wasn't the right time to bring it up. Before this, as the semester wound down and the relationship seemed poised to go either direction, she hadn't been sure that bringing it up would be necessary at all. Now it was clear, however much she dreaded the conversation, it still had to happen.

She looked toward the closed door, toward the sound of the running water and Luke's atonal humming from the shower. In another hour, they would be on the road again, heading for a house by the ocean and a summer free of worry. Then, she thought, she would tell him. When the time was right.

CHAPTER 12

*I*n a small town, there are things you simply grow up knowing. You need them all—the shortcuts, secrets, and scandals that make up the town's collective unconscious, the whispered bits and pieces passed from older lips to younger ears. How you came to know what you know is not important; someone must have told you once. You might even try to think of when, but the details don't come easy. And sometimes, beneath the surface of the local hive mind, there is nothing at all.

Our knowledge has no memory. We have always lived here; what we know has always been.

There has always been a blind spot in the A&P, where the rack of glossy magazines with their too-perfect cover models stands beside a sweating refrigerator case filled with beer, where a green glass longneck can slip undetected into the sleeve of your coat; you know this without knowing how. You know that if you walk into the dense woods behind the soccer field, fifty yards uphill through the crunch and musk of long-dead leaves, you'll find a small but thriving patch of cannabis that no one will admit to planting and nobody will touch. You know that Jennifer Stanton, who sits next to you in trig, calls Tom Stanton "Daddy" but that he is not her father, and that Mrs. Missy Stanton, who used to get so lonely when Tom went on the road, once found a year's company and comfort in the arms of the man who remodeled her kitchen with its sunny yellow wallpaper and tastefully painted woodwork.

And just as you know these things, you know—we knew—that a red Ford tractor with a long-armed front-end loader was hidden in the waters at the south end of Silver Lake.

The tractor had always been there—even though, if you had asked someone, they would grudgingly acknowledge that "always" wasn't quite right. Certainly, there had been a time when there was no tractor. In the days before the lake was found and conceived and built upon as a back-to-nature destination; in the days before "Back to Nature" was a sought-after concept by urbanites who fled the asphalt heat of Boston; in the days before mechanical beasts of burden flattened the land by Silver Lake and cut it into lots, the murky green pool with its topside blanket of iridescent algae and its underwater forest of waving weeds had held water, and nothing more. Then, the lake had been a place to swim and fish, especially fish, where you could rest against the cool, gray rocks that peppered the water's edge, dropping a baited line into the glassy pool.

We called it The Hole—a bad name for a beautiful place. A twisting back road that followed the irregular coast passed over the water here, a small bridge covering the slim gap where the lake squeezed itself between two tall banks, flowed quietly through a water-worn cut bordered by a steep, mossy face of old rock, and emerged into a deep, still, sun-dappled spot bordered on three sides by water-stained granite. Schools of small fish, shimmering sunnies and even some elusive perch, would swim the narrow gauntlet to nibble at the unlucky bugs that skittered on too many legs across the graceful surface. Locals, baited and tackled and armed with small coolers that came full of beer and left full of fish, watched the filament-skinny lines jump and tweak and grow taut, smiled broadly as dinner was hauled in. Small fish, always; even the avid anglers caught nothing larger than a foot, but it didn't matter. The pleasures of solitary casting and the glassy pool and the flapping, gasping, gorgeous catch—these things were ours.

They were ours, until someone else—a self-made millionaire with an eye for development and money to burn—came, and saw, and signed a check that made Silver Lake his.

Even now, nobody can say exactly how the tractor had found its way to its final resting place, hidden under the water in the center of The Hole. Bud Schaeffer, the beer-bellied and flanneled man who had been sitting on it at the time, scratched his head at the bar that night and said, "The brakes just quit, I guess. Shot right out from under me. Shit, LaVerne, I never even knew the godforsaken piece of tin could go that fast." Ten men, the lucky locals who were getting time and a half to clear the land, had seen but could not explain the machine's astonishing arc from the highest bank, where it flew from the edge with its motor still chuffing and a green-brown spray of grass and dirt spiraling from either side, twisted in the air, and gleefully tumbled into the pool. Its spindly plow, with a few stubborn clumps of loose dirt still clinging to its blade, had been the last bit to sink beneath the surface.

The millionaire had been angry, but not too angry—the closeness of the road, the small, steel bridge with its rust-ugly cables, the algae that floated idly on the surface of the water, all meant that the adjacent land would never have fit his vision of the perfect waterfront destination. The best of what he'd bought was still pristine, untouched. And when it was Bud's own equipment that lay at the bottom of the lake . . . well, what could he say? And so they planted a row of saplings back from the edge, to keep any would-be homeowners from investigating the pool too closely, and moved on to the next lot.

"What about your tractor?" the bartender had asked as Bud's ruddy cheeks got redder and his tongue chased brew foam from his upper lip.

"What, that junker?" he slurred. "On its last legs anyhow. Gonna get me a nice new Deere."

"But you gotta get it out of there, right?"

Bud took a last, long swig of his beer, belched loudly, and fixed the bartender with wavery red eyes.

"And just how," he said, elongating each word with drawling sarcasm, "would you propose I do that?"

And so it stayed there, until years had passed and Bud Schaeffer's tractor had become just another thing we grew up knowing. Jennifer Stanton's daddy wasn't her father, the mystery pot beyond the woodside goalpost was not to be touched, and when the lake was running low, if you peered over the side of the south shore bridge, you might just see the reaching tip of that forsaken plow in the green, dark water.

The rest of it, the quiet inlets and piney shoreline path and broad, shimmering, silver center, all were divvied up and closed off behind gated checkpoints—quaint little sentry stations with pretentious security barriers and even more pretentious uniformed guards, who seemed to have been hired based solely on their ability to sneer. But the south shore bridge, already there and maintained by the town, could not be denied to us. And with no other way to escape the summer heat, groups of kids began gathering above The Hole to get in, to get wet, to get in the water in the only way they could.

With the frightened fish long gone and a steel monster slowly rusting beneath its shimmering surface, The Hole still belonged to us.

The day that Brendan Brooks died was the hottest in anyone's memory, so hot that cats lay down in the shade

and panted, elderly women fainted under the weight of
their support hose, and the newly paved parking lot behind
the grocery bubbled and churned and turned into a viscous
black pudding. The sun, silvery-bright and hot, so hot,
blazed arrogantly down from a blanched and cloudless sky.
It baked small bits of gravel into the soft asphalt roads, it
melted popsicles off their sticks and over the grubby hands
of porch-sitting toddlers, and it pounded relentlessly against
the supple skin of the local kids who gathered at the south
shore bridge to cool off.

Brendan could see them from his bedroom window, in
the faux-rustic cabin that sat on the southernmost lot beside
Silver Lake: ten teenaged kids, lithe-limbed boys named
Billy and Jack and Jason, with spindly ribs and small, hard
muscles that made shadows on their sallow backs. He sat
inside, his body bathed in the sweet, chemical cold of the
air conditioner, and watched them—watched as shoes
were shucked off and T-shirts were peeled from sweaty
torsos; watched as each boy clambered onto the rusty,
studded guardrail of the bridge. He watched them, joking
and goading and good-naturedly cussing at each other, until
the bravest of the bunch suddenly gave a whoop and pushed
himself, the muscles of his forearms taut as they lifted his
weight from the ledge, and plummeted feetfirst into the
green, still water below. A moment later, the boy's head
reappeared, hair plastered to his forehead and a wide smile
stretching across his face. His shout echoed in the air.

"C'mon, you chickenshits!"

And then, as Brendan watched with widening eyes,

the boys dropped one by one—shouting in the brief fall from over water to under, emerging elatedly in the frothing channel below the bridge, shoving each other as they grasped and slipped their way back up the bank to do it again.

Brendan, bored and lonely behind the walls of his family's summer retreat, thought he had never seen anything so cool.

Later, behind closed doors and over a coffee-stained folding table at the police station, ten terrified kids and one inconsolable woman knit the two ends of the story together: how he'd called out his plan to walk down to the bridge; how his mother, watching the local boys splashing safely down in the cool water, had given her reluctant okay; how he had appeared, tentative but smiling, fifteen and fresh faced and wearing an old T-shirt that said "Blame Canada" on it.

He had waved at the sneering entry guard and trotted toward the group at the bridge, his scuffed sneakers kicking up small clouds of roadside dirt. He had said "Hey," and then nothing else, had just watched them for a while, his freckled face full of friendly curiosity and even a little amazement as the boys continued splashing down and climbing up.

They had been surprised by his interest, still more surprised when he stayed and watched and, finally, began asking questions.

"Is it deep?"

"Deep enough," they replied.

"Is it cold?"

"Nah," they said.

And then, in a move that might have gone so far as to bridge the gap between the locals and the summerers had things not come to such a horrible, heartbreaking end, Brendan Brooks asked if he could jump, too, and the boys at the bridge just shrugged.

And made room for him.

He did as he'd seen them do, when he was still only watching them from the other side of the guarded entrance— peeling off his T-shirt, kicking off his shoes, taking his place in the perching row on the guardrail. To the drivers that passed on the bridge behind them, even to the boys themselves, he was indistinguishable from the rest of the group, just one more lithe young man with wiry muscles and a farmer's tan and a couple inches of plaid-patterned boxer waistband sticking above the top hem of his shorts. One of them, or so close to, that it no longer mattered that his life—his home, in a place full of city grit and noise and high-rise luxury—was so far in distance and experience from Bridgeton that the boys he sat beside couldn't have pictured it if you asked them to. He waited there, the sun baking hard and hot against his bare shoulders, his nose tickled by the hot tarry scent of the road and the vague still-water stench of the lake, until a few more jumpers had disappeared into the water and one of them, treading in the murky green below, called back.

"Hey, new guy! You jumping or what?"

Later, the boys all agreed that Brendan hadn't hesitated for so much as a second. A broad smile broke through his composed demeanor, he nodded confidently at the heckler, and then he dropped.

And when he came to the surface, shaking water out of his eyes and raising a mock-celebratory fist in the air, he had still been grinning.

Things could have happened so differently, the afternoon wearing away on a path that didn't lead to tragedy. It almost did; an hour passed while the boys jumped and climbed the banks to jump again, and everyone was getting hungry, and the sun had reluctantly sunk to a more comfortable place behind a row of tall pines that cast their spindly shadows over the bridge in dark, sheer ribbons. It was almost time to go. They were jumping less frequently now, a few of them choosing instead to lean against the guardrail and smoke cigarettes, letting their skin dry comfortably in the late-afternoon heat. Nobody took much notice.

They saw, but did not see, the new kid—padding barefoot to the other side of the bridge, peering over the edge into The Hole.

Brendan's eyes had widened, the way that eyes do when they fall on something never before seen, a place made by nature, beautiful and fresh and far beyond anything city constructed out of stone and steel. The perfect circle of dark, still water; the overhanging trees rising gracefully around it; the cool, gray boulders worn smooth by time and weather—Brendan saw all of this and gasped at its beauty.

And then, smiling with the joy of his discovery, he had climbed nimbly over the guardrail.

It could have been different—if the tallest boy, the one with the high cheekbones and shock of shaggy hair, the one who, back then, still had a mother to run home to at the end of the day, had looked up from lighting his cigarette only a moment sooner. If Brendan himself had said something— "Watch this," or "Check it out," or any of the other things that boys say to each other before they take that jump. If, if, if.

Instead, the eyes of the group fell on him moments too late. They saw him standing on the other side, standing on the side where nobody went to jump, not ever, because everybody knows that on that side of the bridge you do not jump. They felt that something was wrong, and without knowing exactly why, one boy stood quickly and stretched out a hand and, in a voice so strange and quiet that he didn't even recognize it as his own, said, "Wait."

He might have paused; he might not. They could only say that if he had, it had been for only a moment—not long enough to stop him, not long enough even to say *Wait, wait,* again. And still smiling, he had leaped into space.

The sound of the splash roused the rest of the group, fell on their ears as cause for alarm before they could even remember why. Why, despite the beauty and lure of The Hole's deep center, they did not jump—*you do not jump*— from that side. Why the sight of the rippling water with its light scrum of bobbing algae filled their mouths with the cold, coppery taste of dread. Why the sound of the splash had carried with it something else, a terrifying final note that clung to the rush of water and air, a faraway thunk that sounded like metal.

The place where Brendan had disappeared was covered with froth, a wide white fissure in the water that slowed as they watched, as ripples from his entry broke with quiet slaps against the bank, until no more ripples came. A wide honeycomb of small bubbles floated on the surface, bursting one by one. The water became green-black and silent and still once more. It closed like glass, a seamless window that let nothing in and nothing out, and on the bridge above, nobody breathed.

Far away, a motorboat droned idly across the lake.

Below the surface, inside a blooming cloud of crimson, two green eyes peeled sightlessly toward the sun.

And then, slicing the golden afternoon air like a knife, came the sound of Brendan's mother screaming.

AMELIA

*L*uke was in high spirits as they sped up the ramp to I-95, reaching for her hand as they entered Connecticut and loudly announcing, "Welcome to the whitest state in America!"

She laughed and turned to look out the window. The afternoon had been gray, with a few drops of rain falling sporadically on the windshield, but now the clouds overhead seemed to be breaking. They looked stretched, thinned out and tufted with pink tendrils that reached back and to the west where the sun was beginning to set. It reflected off the rearview mirror, painting a bright wash of orange light onto her neck and chin. A cold, damp wind blew through the window—coming from far away, from an ocean she couldn't see, but which she knew the road would follow all the way there, to the Cape, where they would follow a series of roundabouts and finally wind their way to the small, clapboard house that was theirs for the summer. The breeze licked at her upper arms. Luke, in a moment of uncharacteristic but entertaining vulgarity, had said he liked the way the thin jersey dress she'd chosen for traveling clung to her tits, but now she shivered and wished she'd remembered to pull a sweater from her duffel bag. It was impossible now, locked in the trunk and out of reach.

He seemed to have read her thoughts as he shrugged out of his hooded sweatshirt and handed it over to her. "Here, put this on," he said.

"What are you, psychic?" she asked, smiling. She draped the sweatshirt over her front, like a blanket, and tucked her knees up beneath it. It smelled deliciously male, a mix of sweat and deodorant clinging to the soft fabric.

"As a matter of fact, I am," he said, laughing. "But in this case, it was my highly developed sense of touch which informed me that you were shivering hard enough to shake the entire car."

"Oh, ha-ha," she said. "You must be disappointed, you can't see my tits anymore."

He looked over at her and breathed an exaggerated sigh. "Alas, I cannot. But it's all right."

"You forgive me?"

"Well, there will be other days, and other drives, and"—he paused for a moment—"other tits."

Then, "Hey, don't hit me! I'm driving!"

She settled back, still laughing and glaring at him in pretend-fury, and tucked her hands under the hoodie again. The setting sun had filled the car with orange light, pouring through the back window and bathing the dashboard in a wash of color. They grinned at each other as the sun finally slipped below the horizon. Ahead, the gray highway with its sleek dotted line stretched into the distance, nothing but asphalt and trees and one garish green sign that announced a service area five miles ahead.

She slumped deeper into the seat and sighed.

"You okay?"

"I feel sleepy," she said. "Which is all your fault."

Luke pounded his chest exaggeratedly and grunted, then grinned and turned his eyes back toward the road. She looked at him, not sure whether to be amused or amazed. He seemed to become more relaxed the more they drove, the further they got from their old lives as college students and the closer they came to their new ones as . . . well, whatever they would become.

It wasn't just that he was relaxed, she realized. Everything about him was different—he looked confident, eager, in-the-moment.

He looked happy.

She hated to spoil it.

Back at his parents' place, she had almost told him. Now she scolded herself for being a coward, for lacking the guts to just say what needed to be said, for even worrying about how he might react. It was her life, she thought. Her future. And in her dreams for that future, she had never wanted anything so passionately as she wanted this. If he was able to put aside his own agenda, the cohabitation-and-consumerism plan he seemed to have decided on, then he'd be able to see how important it was. And if he really loved her, he'd be able to forget about the plan. To improvise a little, to take a chance on a different life. He could, at the very least, be happy for her.

And if he couldn't . . . at least she would know, without a doubt, what kind of man he really was.

Luke's voice cut into her thoughts.

"We need gas," he said, easing off the accelerator and allowing the car to drift toward the off-ramp. Ahead, she could see the floodlights and neon of the roadside station, hear the rumble of heavy trucks.

"Oh, let me contribute," she said. She reached into her purse, fumbling for the silver cigarette case that held her cash.

"I can't believe you're still using that thing," Luke said, shaking his head and smiling. "Haven't you ever wanted a wallet?"

"Why, because they're so much better?" she said, pulling the case free and rapping him lightly on the forehead with it.

"They're certainly less painful," he replied.

It was just minutes later, with the needle on the gas gauge pushing just past the F mark, when he suddenly turned to her—smiling broadly, his eyes alight like a kid at Christmastime.

"This feels great," he said. "Being on the road, it's fucking great. I feel like I could drive all night, I'm so excited." He turned to look at her again. "Are you excited?"

"Yes," she answered honestly. "I am."

CHAPTER 13

On the day that they arrested the men from Silver Lake, the rust-covered plow of the infamous tractor appeared above the surface, standing like a small sentry dead center in the black shimmering maw of The Hole. That same morning, the announcement came that mandatory water restrictions would be in effect for the month of August. The lake had retreated by inches, disappearing downward every day, and the summer people—affected at last—looked worriedly out at the shrinking pool and feared with the same gnawing panic as the rest of us. Feared that murder had slipped through the gates, that something evil was lying in wait on the lake bottom, drinking the water away. It slipped and sloshed lower on the rocks, and lower still, exposing things long hidden in the shadowy murk and waving shoreline weeds. It revealed old grudges and older graffiti, small spats over property lines and prime dockage, petty insults and four-letter words scratched angrily into dock posts or the glittering granite rocks. On the day that the police blazed through the gates of Silver Lake, the water had dipped so low that a seventy-two-year-old man, out for his morning swim, stopped and stared in amazement at two grime-covered sculptures with pointy red hats lying in the newly exposed muck below his neighbor's dock. His garden gnomes had gone missing the previous year; at the time, the family next door had pleaded ignorance and blamed the theft on local pranksters.

Beneath the surface, we weren't so different after all.

And two hours later, the Bridgeton police sped through the sentried gates, pulled into the flagstone drive of a four-bedroom cottage on the waterfront, pulled three never-used firearms from their snug leather holsters, and, with to-the-letter efficiency, placed two of its residents under arrest.

With the news rippling like scattershot through our phone lines and knocking urgently at our front door in the form of hovering neighbors, my mother locked the house tightly in spite of the heat, slammed four Advil down her throat, and fell heavily into one of the creaky kitchen chairs.

"If that phone rings one more time," she said, the last three words carrying a warning edge that made no additional explanation necessary. A butter knife lay on the table; she picked it up and gestured threateningly at the handset. In the place where it had been, a gob of grease still clung to the tablecloth, but Mom didn't seem to notice it. Lately, I thought, she didn't seem to notice anything; I would come home from the restaurant to find breakfast's crumb-covered dishes still piled on the countertop, glasses filled with lukewarm water and condensation rings drying on the tablecloth, the milk left out to spoil. I had struggled through July like a zombie, detached and half dead, pushing against the sensation that I had become a ghost in my own life. Now, brought halfway back to earth by James and Lindsay and the restless and inexorable pull of townie gossip, I looked at the oily gob of butter and realized that my mother might be even more checked-out than me. The evil that had arrived on our doorsteps that summer had moved inside here, too—it was living in our kitchen, poisoning the food with strange rot, whispering to her from just inside the pantry door.

From the corner of my eye, I could see the hulking, overstuffed shape of the recycling bin. I didn't need to look to know that it was full, brimming with the piled green-glass curves of empty wine bottles.

"What's going on?" I said, realizing at the same time that I knew well enough, realizing that I only wanted her to talk to me.

"They've arrested two of those obnoxious men from Silver Lake," my mother said. She looked out the window, squinting her eyes against the brightness outside. I could see the hangover headache beating small pulses against her hairline. "You know the ones—that group, they tried to close the bridge after that kid died. Concerned Citizens of whatever-it-is."

"Concerned Citizens of Silver Shoals," I said. I'd seen

them at the restaurant—the same height, same build, all with the same nondescript fortyish face. They walked in heavy-step unison. They were a small army of cloned mediocrity. They'd come on the scene after Brendan's death; I remembered the Chief of Police, standing on our porch in the fading twilight and staring down the street, angry sweat sheening on his bald pate.

"Idiots!" he'd snapped. "Concerned citizens, can you believe that crap? 'Citizens,' my ass. And don't even get me started on *shoals*, for the love of Pete, these moneyed sons of bitches don't even know what a goddamn shoal goddamn is."

My father, lending an ear to his longtime friend, stood in the shadows near the door with his jaw set and an edge in his voice. "What do you plan to do about it?"

The chief, head shaking slowly—as much in disbelief as anger—sighed and said, "These people, they've got no business telling us what to do with our own damned bridge. Or anything else. Let them sit out a winter here, work an overnight shift at the plant, and maybe then I'll listen to their goddamn opinions on community safety."

And then, in a move that might have been funny had it not betrayed so much barely contained anger, the Chief of Police had cocked his head to one side and spat on the sidewalk.

"Shoals," my mother echoed, grinning slightly in shared memory of the chief's fury. "That's it."

"You know what people are going to say," I replied. I slid into the chair next to her. "They've been rabid about the dead girl. That was them at the street fair, too—that fight."

She snickered; she knew the story. In truth, the whole thing had lasted less than a minute—just enough time for one of the men to cause a small commotion by accusing the entire town of incompetence, and for Tom to step outside, listen for a moment, and then cleanly break his nose with one punch.

I cleared my throat. "Some people think one of them did it."

"Definitely not."

I pushed back. "How do you know?"

"Well, your father and I do still talk to each other occasionally." She sighed. "And according to him, it's just not possible. The police have been in there more than once, and nobody's ever seen that girl."

We sat together in silence, my mother with her fingertips pressed against the papery, translucent skin of her temples, rubbing small circles into the spot just before her hairline. Outside, the sun passed momentarily behind a cloud; the light in the kitchen turned drab and shadowless.

I turned over the few known facts about the murder in my head, feeling the hairs on the back of my neck rise up as I thought of the body lying in the morgue. Cold, alone, unclaimed—maybe forever. No resolution, no closure. An unburied body in slow decay. A patch of isolated road where, no matter how hard it rained, the pavement was always stained the faintest shade of red.

Something horrible, something that usually stayed safely

outside and away from the quiet comfort of Bridgeton, had moved into town and would never, ever leave.

On the tabletop, the phone chirped once and then began to ring. I snatched it and pressed it to my stomach, wanting to muffle the noise. My mom buried her head in her hands as I slipped out the kitchen door, lifting the handset to my ear as it swung shut behind me.

"Hello?"

"Becca?" James's voice was so high and tense that I cringed away, wincing.

I held it several inches from my head and muttered, "It's me, I'm here."

His breathing was hard and fast, as though he'd run for the phone and dialed in a hurry. Something was wrong.

"James? What's going on?"

The words came out in an unpunctuated tumble. "Have you heard what happened?"

The air left my lungs in a huff of disbelief, as inside, the rational me rolled her eyes.

"Wait a minute," I said. "This is a gossip call? You scared the shit out of m—"

"So you know?" he said, his voice still alive with tension and worry.

"This isn't news, you know," I said. "You didn't exactly get the jump on this."

"*Becca*—"

"Yes, okay?" I spat. "Yes, I know they arrested two of those jerks from the lake."

"But people are saying they did it," he said. "You know, that they killed that girl. And—"

"People are panicking, that's all. They just want it solved."

"But the police arrested those guys," he said. "I mean, that happened. They're at the station now."

"Yeah, for some reason that has nothing to do with killing anyone," I said.

"Like what?" he countered.

I sighed. "I don't know. I mean, hell, did you hear about that old guy's garden gnomes? Maybe they did *that*."

There was a brief pause and then James started laughing, just a little at first, then harder as the tension and anxiety in his voice disappeared. I started cackling too, grateful beyond words to find that we could still share a moment that was light and loose and . . .

Normal, I thought. *There it is.*

As my breathing slowed and settled, as I waited for James to get back under control, the thought I'd nearly had before came floating back to the surface. The men arrested that morning had no hand in the murder, but part of me stubbornly insisted that there was something else. Something missed, something misplaced.

"So I guess you heard your version of this from a reliable source." James had stopped laughing; I heard him light up a cigarette, the spark and hiss of the match-flame echoing in the empty space after his question.

"Mother via father," I said. "Does that count as reliable?"

"Sure," he said. "Especially by comparison."

"Why, who'd you hear from?"

"Craig."

I blinked. In my head, the half-formed thought of something missing suddenly burned bright and hot.

Something horrible had arrived on our doorsteps this summer.

Or someone.

"Craig," I repeated.

"Yeah." He paused. "I was helping him out today, moving some of his grandma's stuff. He went out to get beer and came back all hopped up about how some of those guys were arrested."

"I'll bet he was," I said.

"What's that supposed to mean?"

"Nothing, I just—"

"You had a tone," James said.

"Sorry," I replied, hurriedly. "It's just . . . you know. He talks about it a lot. The dead girl, the murder."

I could hear James's shrug. "Like you said, everyone wants to know what happened."

"Yeah, but . . ." I paused, measuring my words. "He's a little more interested than most. And what he said, about finding something—"

"Just a joke, Becca," he said quickly. "Remember?"

I let out an exasperated sigh. Why did he have to have an answer for everything? There was silence from the other end, and then a thin exhalation as James blew smoke away from the receiver.

"Listen," he said, "I hear you. I do. But you've got to know, whatever you're thinking about Craig, you're wrong."

It was my turn to sigh with exasperation.

"Look, I'm just saying—"

"Yeah, and maybe you should think about what you're 'just saying.'" He spat the word out hard, urgently. "I don't know what you think Craig did, but whatever it is, I can promise you he *didn't*. You may not trust him, but can you trust me, at least? I know he's not the type to be involved in something like this. And in this town, it could be really bad if somebody started saying that he was. Really bad."

I stayed quiet. In the kitchen, I heard a clatter and thump as my mother stumbled against the table. A full minute passed before he spoke again.

"Look, Becca, I understand what you're saying. I know you're worried. And I'll talk to him. Okay? Just let me handle it," he said. "Promise me you'll let me handle it, and you won't say anything."

"James—"

"Promise me, Becca. Please."

If I closed my eyes, I could see him there. The phone pressed to his ear, his voice echoing in the near-empty house as he waited for me to give my word. I could see the three o'clock light slanting through the windows, the dust on the furniture, the broken boards on the porch. A warm breeze would blow lightly from the west, weaving its way between the trees, passing over the surface of the small pond and through the place, just behind the house, where there had once been a garden.

Years ago, that wind would have caressed the sharp purple spears of the clematis blossoms or shaken the golden pollen from the bobbing, heavy-petaled peonies; now, with everything gone to seed, it touched only the things that could still survive when left to fend for themselves. The wind carried news of the plants that thrived alone, forgotten and uncared-for. It swept through with the smell of the water, the pungent musk of pondweed, the dark notes of earth and leaves.

It was a year ago that I'd stood there, shifting my weight uncertainly on the porch steps. James had appeared like a ghost and waved at me from behind the dirty gray glass of the storm door. One pane was missing completely, others shattered but intact with their surfaces cut clean through by a patchwork web of silver lines. Behind, the sharp angles of his face were visible only in oblong, broken slices.

It was his father who damaged the door, he told me. Running in from the garden at the sound of James's strangled cries, slipping in the mud at the base of the porch, vaulting up the sagging stairs in twos and threes and pounding down the hallway into the dayroom—a room full of sobbing and sunlight and everything else but the ragged sandpaper dragging of his wife's shallow breath. The crochet coverlet that wrapped her wasted body lay perfectly still and flat against her chest. She was gone.

Later, they would find the hinges torn loose from their splintering anchors, three panes of glass cracked; another, low and on the left, had disappeared entirely.

"We never found the pieces from this one," he had said,

looking over his shoulder and smiling with so much covered misery that it made my stomach hurt.

"Weird," I said. I ducked underneath his arm, draping its heavy length over my shoulder and resting my head against his chest.

"The paramedics probably kicked it away," he said, his eyes fixed on a place behind us and down the steps, seeing the path that her body had followed as it was wheeled from the house, prone on a stretcher with a sheet pulled tight over her gaunt, gray face. They had called for an ambulance, not knowing what else to do, forcing James to stand on the porch and wait for the white bus with its strobing band of electric red lights to trundle up the drive. He had been the one to walk to the driver's-side window, his shoulders hunched and face contorted with grief, and explain to the surprised EMTs in their clean khaki uniforms that they could take their time. There was nobody here to save.

Beyond the bone-white outline of the faded wood, through the place where there should have been glass but wasn't, a dust-shrouded banister lined the stairs to the second floor. The places where fingertips had pressed against the wood gleamed like oil, three- and four-pronged marks that trailed sharply upward and then disappeared. There were photographs on the ascending wall, pictures of a brooding, little-boy version of James. He was running through a pumpkin patch, a look of intense concentration on his small, serious face. He was seated on the lap of an elderly woman with veiny hands, skin like old tissue paper, coffee-stained teeth that were flashing in a broad, uneven smile. He was here, in this house, on this stairway, with his mother's long shadow darkening the wall beside him.

I could still remember that photograph. In it, he was turned toward the place where she had been standing, beyond the reach of the camera's eye. His face was an open shout of delight at the surprise, Mommy, whose body was blocking the light that poured through the east-facing window, whose curly hair was casting a tendril shadow over the toe of his sneaker. It could break your heart, if you looked too long—at the shadow, at the tiny face with eyes alight and open mouth, at the gleaming woodwork and unfaded wallpaper and sweet white dabs of sunlight that played on the floor. There had been a home here, polished and scrubbed, cared for. There had been a family. There had been love, and patches of light on the stairs. There had been a time before everything turned gray.

"Aren't you worried about this?" I'd asked, standing on the porch and trailing my finger along the inner groove where the missing glass had been. "Somebody could come in . . ."

I looked back at the endless trees, the uninterrupted forest, as James smiled sadly.

"There's nobody out here. That was why she liked it. It's quiet; it's private. My mom grew up in the city, did I ever tell you that? She grew up in New York, and she was always saying—" his voice suddenly broke and he stopped short, swallowed hard. His shaggy hair—unkempt, uncut, longer than a mother would have liked—fell over his eyes as he looked toward the ground and muttered, "Sorry."

It had still been early, then. We were still only skimming the surface of "together," still learning each other's tics, getting to know the nuances of expression and tone that were second nature to me now. Then, I had been uncomfortable and the moment passed with needling self-consciousness, him swallowing so hard and often that his Adam's apple bobbed under his skin as though it were alive, me rubbing his back in awkward circles and beginning to sweat with the pressure to say something. Anything. At times like this, and there had been more than one, I felt that his mother was there—standing to the side, watching us, all mournful eyes and slow-shaking head that this trespassing girl was here, on her front porch, in her private forest, and could not even comfort her son.

Finally, he had cleared his throat, and blinked, and said, "Anyway, we don't worry about someone coming in. There's nothing in here that anybody cares about."

And I had held his hand, and touched his shoulder, and wondered what kind of hopelessness he must have felt—to make himself part of that nothing.

CHAPTER 14

On the morning of the arrests, exactly one month to the day after Amelia Anne Richardson's body had made its prostrate pilgrimage from the dirty and dusty roadside to the cold, clean interior of the morgue, a dark, heavy wall of mounting cloud had appeared above the western mountains. A rising wind, insistent and tinged with the damp promise of a late July thunderstorm, blew coldly down the quiet streets and brushed its clammy fingers against the limp faces of the parched and shuddering leaves. The sun grew unsure of itself and fled the sky. Inside, people tiptoed through the tepid indoors of their carpeted hallways, stepped over their thresholds into the moving air, and sighed with relief at the promise of rain.

For a few short hours, it seemed that the unsettling presence of murder, mystery, and irreversible change that had haunted our streets all summer would finally, finally be washed away.

The news blew into town before the second set of handcuffs had clicked into place around the beefy, blue-veined wrists of the suspects, picking up speed as it raced through phone lines and over hedges, banging through front doors, barging into kitchens where it surprised families in the midst of their unhurried Sunday breakfasts. It rushed eagerly down the streets, richocheting off the bare, sun-faded faces of stately white homes and wrapping in a breathless tangle around the trunks of old trees. Beneath the austere ceiling of the hilltop Presbyterian church, gossip skipped up and down the aisle and murmured in the spaces between the worn wood pews, until the black-cloaked pastor, his flushed face and thinning hair grown shiny and damp with frustrated perspiration, paused midsermon and said, "Excuse me, but I must insist that the noise stop immediately."

Later, long after the speculation had given way to sad and dissatisfying truth, it was discovered that three words had been scribbled in the margins of one of the ancient church hymnals. The hasty ink bled its black accusation back through ten parchment-thin pages, the letters growing fainter and then disappearing entirely on page one hundred and fifty-seven, just beside the first verse of "My Soul in Silence Waits for God."

IT WAS THEM.

It had to be them. We knew it, we all did—the

neighbors who talked from the sides of their mouths, the women who waited until the kids had gone to bed before phoning a friend to trade theories, the beer drinkers in the East Bank Tavern who turned on their stools, glasses raised, and toasted the untrustworthiness of outsiders. Because in a town like this, there were the people who belonged, and the ones who didn't. And the dead girl, the one with skin like clean white paper and expensive highlights in her blood-soaked hair—that girl wasn't one of us. If you had asked anyone, anyone at all, we'd have told you as much in a heartbeat. And who had killed her? Who could have? Who would have?

Them.

And just as they had done before, just as they always did, people came together and talked about what they'd always known.

Because there had always been something wrong with the summerers. They were too snide, too snobby, too suspiciously ready to throw their money at substandard lakefront property in a town with no real cachet. They talked to us using short sentences and slow language, pandering to grown men as though they were stupid children. Until they wanted something; then, they seeded their speech with four-syllable words and hoped that the lies in between would slip by unnoticed. They had driven up the prices in the grocery with their demands for imported foods, organic vegetables, strangely shaped and weird-smelling artisanal cheese that none of the locals would touch. They had cheated someone's cousin out of his rightful claim to a lakefront lot. They had built those guarded gates and chosen the narrow-eyed assholes who staffed them. They called us "boy" and "hey, you" and "dear," called us "honey" and "sweetie" in voices that rang with condescension and held no kindness.

They had always wanted to take what wasn't theirs.

They had taken that poor girl's life.

But better that it should end like this—when the guilty men were cuffed, dragged, shoved into the backseats of two police cruisers, and everyone knew the reasons why.

"He had an affair with her," people said.

"She was obsessed."

"She threatened to tell his wife."

He had dragged her into the dark and savaged her there by the side of the road. He had hit her with a pipe, with a rock, with the bare blunt force of his dirty fists. Or that it had been both of them; they had raped her together, or one at a time, one man holding her thin arms while the other tore her dignity to shreds. It was a conspiracy. It was a reluctant cover-up. It was cold-blooded murder with a side of blackmail. Don't say that I told you, but you can trust me.

I heard it from someone who knows.

Later, when the the truth came out—when it turned out that the men from Silver Lake were guilty not of murder, but of taking it upon themselves to beat the living shit out of a caramel-skinned landscaper who'd looked, as they later told the police, "suspicious"—the same eager souls who had excitedly spread rumors of resolution through the cool, breezy morning were finally forced to redial, recant, admit that the real story had been anything but. The sun reappeared with blazing strength in the five o'clock sky. It baked the sidewalks and streets until the heat rose in thick, shimmering waves and each blade of grass bowed its slender neck in dazed submission. It sucked in the air and spit it back at us, lung-clogging hot. People stepped outside, looked to the west with longing, and recognized the familiar deadweight of murder in the unmoving air. The sky was bare, the clouds vanished. The earth was cracking, and Amelia Anne Richardson's body grew colder, drier, deader, in its anonymous plastic shroud.

And murder, standing just inside the open door, leaned closer and whispered, "It will never rain again."

AMELIA

She woke with a start, curled up against the car door with the handle digging uncomfortably into her armpit. There had been a sound—some sort of bell, or chime—that had cut through her sleep, and she looked around for the source before remembering where she was. Outside the window, lit by the ghostly light of the high beams, were the gnarled trunks of tall trees. They waved lightly in the night breeze.

She was alone.

The car was stopped, silent, the keys dangling from the ignition, the driver's-side door yawning open with nothing but impenetrable blackness beyond. The skin on her arms prickled and then broke out in gooseflesh as she stared at the empty driver's seat, her mind pushing aside the cobwebs of sleep when she realized, with growing clarity and a sense of alarm, that she could not see Luke. Struggling out of her seat belt and shrugging off his sweatshirt, she fumbled with the door handle.

Behind her, there was a thudding sound. Someone had slammed the trunk shut. Crunching footsteps came next, moving around the car, and then Luke's face suddenly appeared in the black emptiness beyond the door, his lips pulled back in a self-satisfied smile. In the yellowish light of the interior, they looked dirty—slimy, like rocks that had been sitting too long in still water.

Gross, she thought, and then felt immediately guilty for it. He had let her sleep while he drove them all the way here, hours of navigating alone in the dark, and that was on top of the drive from school to his family's home in New York. God, he had been behind the wheel steadily for—she looked at the clock.

And then snapped to attention.

"Luke, where are we? We can't possibly be there yet, it's too early."

He kept smiling, his face looming like a pale moon in the corner of the open door. "That's my math wiz," he grinned. "I just had to make one more stop on the way."

"One more— what's going on?"

"Come outside."

"I need to put my shoes back on," she said, fumbling for them. One of them seemed to leap out of her hand when she touched it, diving away beneath the seat.

"Come on," he urged, and disappeared. She saw him cross around the front of the car, the headlights sweeping his body as he passed through them. He beckoned again, still smiling.

She eyed him suspiciously, but complied. The breeze kissed her arms and neck as the door swung open, pressing the loose fabric of her dress tight around her body. Luke turned and walked away, striding past the glow of the headlights and into the dark beyond.

She winced as she unbent her knees, uncurling stiffly and putting her feet uncertainly on the ground.

"Ame?" Luke's voice floated out of the dark.

"Coming!" she called.

Small rocks skittered away under her feet as she stepped carefully along the thin white beam from the headlight, her eyes adjusting slowly to the dark. There were trees here, hundreds of them, sailing up and away into a sky that looked like it was littered with tiny jewels.

She gasped and craned her neck to take it all in. There were so many stars, an incredible patchwork of glittering light in the blue-black openness above, more stars than she had ever seen. For years, her night skies had been filled with the orangey glare of city lights, skies in which only two or three points of light could ever break through the electric ambiance and low-hanging smog. In this sky, they were everywhere—as common and numerous as grains of sand.

It was only when she had lowered her chin, allowing the air to rush back into her nostrils, that she realized she could not smell the ocean. Wherever they were, it felt *inland*, surrounded on all sides by these trees, the night air loamy with the scent of earth, and something else . . . something sweet. Something heavy, floral, that seemed to float out of the trees and drape itself around her neck, tangling in her hair, caressing her face, and begging to be adored.

She could see him, now, standing just ahead. There was an opening, a sense of air and space, and she saw that he was standing just back from a ledge that overlooked the country-side below. Miles away and to the east, a loose grid of soft little lights seemed to be nestled comfortably in the trees.

A town—a tiny one—surrounded by miles of blackness.

"This must be beautiful in the daytime," she said, stepping up to stand beside him.

"It is," he replied. He put an arm around her shoulders, squeezed briefly, and turned to look at her. In the ambient light from the car and the cold, barely there glow of starlight, she saw him as a series of features—the straight, patrician nose; the unblinking eyes; the grim, tense line of his mouth.

"I used to come here when I was a kid," he said. He dropped his hand from her shoulders and pushed it deep into his pocket, hunching his shoulders against a nonexistent wind. "My parents had a place, for awhile, on this lake. Silver Lake. It's down there, you could see it now if it weren't so dark." He paused, frowning. "We should have left earlier. I wanted to be here at sunset."

She watched him, half smiling. The idea of Luke as a little boy—a little, lake-house-having boy—amused her. She had always seen him as a child of extreme privilege, someone who took it for granted that each summer would be spent at the Cape, that each winter would bring a trip to Aspen or Jackson Hole. It fit his rigid nature; the idea that there was just one right way to live life, visiting the right places, knowing the right people.

He was watching her, waiting for a response. She shrugged. "Sorry, sweetheart. If I'd known—"

He shook his head. "No, no, I'm not saying it's your fault. Of course you didn't know." He turned to look out at the vista, the endless patches of dark-on-dark-on-darker, the sweet sprinkling of lights that twinkled back amiably in the night.

"That's a town," he said, pointing. "It's been a while, but I remember it was really small. Quaint, I guess—it's got a quaint name, Bridgedale or . . . no, that's not right. But something like that. You'd probably like it."

"I probably would," she replied. "But—"

"Anyway," he rushed in, cutting her off, and she was glad in the dark that he couldn't see her rolling her eyes, "anyway, I brought you here because . . . um. Because I really liked it here. My family used to have picnics up here, back when we still had the house, and we saw my dad a lot more then . . ."

She nodded but began to tune him out, listening to him ramble about the meaningfulness of this place—*Geez, Luke, you're not the only one with a cute family who did cute things*—when he suddenly grabbed her hand.

"And I know things have been a little tense between us for the past few weeks," he said, squeezing her hand. "But that's over now. We're all done with college, and now we can move on from all that stuff, you know?"

"Mm-hmm," she said, squeezing back.

He barely seemed to hear her, talking faster now, "I was so worried all the time with all the studying, all those exams, and then trying to figure out about a job—well, I mean, all of it, I was just so stressed. But now it's time to move on from that, and you won't be so busy with the acting thing, that's all done for you," and he squeezed her hand again.

She didn't squeeze back.

He didn't notice.

"That's kid stuff," he said, "just kid stuff, and we've moved past it. And I love you, Ame, and I want to keep . . . well, moving on. With you. So, um—" he let go of her hand, which was damp with his sweat, and began fumbling in his pocket.

Oh, no.

"I wanted to ask you—"

Her head had begun to shake, very slightly, back and forth.

Oh no, no, no.

"—if you would—"

Please, no. No, no, no.

He dropped to his knee. Even in the weak light, she could see the ring clutched in his fingers. There was the thin circle of gleaming gold, there was the square stone mounted high and proud on top. Glinting, glittering, cold and hard and embarrassingly big.

"—marry me," he finished.

"I want you to be my wife."

CHAPTER 15

"*I* will come back," he'd said.

It had been nearly a week.

"Just wait," he'd said, his voice full of tenderness, now that I'd promised to let him handle it. "I'm going to New York, to see my aunt. I have to . . . we still have my mom's jewelry. I'm bringing it to her."

There had been silence, then, the sound of his breath in the receiver, the sound of flint striking and another cigarette being lit.

"And you can keep yourself busy in the meantime."

"Busy?" I said.

"Only two weeks left, right? You're leaving in September. Don't you need to pack?"

I'd tried to speak and couldn't. My focus went to a spot on the floor, where I pushed the toe of my sneaker against the baseboard.

"I'm not sure anymore," I said, finally.

"*Becca*—"

"Don't say my name like that," I interrupted, fighting against the urge to snap. "Don't act like I'm a silly girl. I'm not. I've thought about this more than you can imagine."

"Baby," he said, and my eyes pricked with tears at the tenderness in the nickname. "It's not that I wouldn't want you to be here with me. I mean, God, that's all I wanted for the longest time. I thought—"

He stopped abruptly.

"So what changed?" I whispered, hating the desperation in my voice. Through the phone, with miles in between us, he sounded small and far away.

"I just want you to think about what you'd do . . . if I wasn't here."

Inside my head, a sly voice had cooed words I did not want to hear. *Stupid girl*, it said, *you see? He's making plans without you.*

I swallowed, closed my eyes and tried to force it away.

"Where else would you be?" I said.

Quiet. The house creaked around me, and I heard James sigh.

"Nowhere, Becca. Nowhere."

I threw myself into work. Extra hours, double shifts, arriving early to set up the dining room and staying late to wipe each surface clean. I watched Craig slug beers at the bar, brazen, while Lindsay danced flirtatiously around him. I had served and bused and brought drink after drink to waiting diners, and tried not to picture James, alone on the road. It worked, until one afternoon when I banged through the door of the kitchen only to have Tom step heavily into my path.

"Don't you ever take a day off?" he asked, smiling.

"Nope," I smirked back, and tried to step around him.

He moved with me.

"Yes," he said. His smile had faded; there were lines of concern around his mouth. "Today, this is your day off."

"No," I said, too loudly. Tom's eyebrows shot up, but I couldn't stop. He didn't understand. I needed this—the heavy weight of the trays and the comforting scent of bread, the well-worn path from the front of the house to the kitchen and back. The predictable rhythm of Lindsay's giggly chatter. The sense, just for a few hours, that I knew exactly who I was and what I was doing and that there was nothing, not a single thing, to be afraid of.

"I need to be here," I insisted, hearing the edge of panic creep into my voice. Tom's eyebrows knit together and he placed a meaty hand on my shoulder.

"Honey," he said, his voice warm and paternal, "even if you didn't need a break—and you do—I've gotta get the new girl in here for training. If she's taking your place, she needs to walk the floor for at least a couple days, y'know?"

I stared at him, not understanding. He smiled and clapped me on the back.

"Don't look so glum! In just a couple weeks, you'll be outta here forever!"

As I plodded back to my car, I heard his voice behind me.

"Hey," he called. I looked back, desperate, stupid hope all over my face.

Tom was leaning out the door, displaying a smile that carried a hint of puzzlement. "It's not really forever," he said. "The job's all yours for next summer, if you want it!"

Next summer.

I couldn't even begin to picture it, couldn't imagine anything beyond the edge of the yard, the dead heat of another day, the cloying taste of sweet, cheap wine as it dripped down my throat. The bottle in my hand sloshed again, another crimson droplet freeing itself from the slick green rim and landing on my sleeve.

It looked like blood.

Blood in the dirt by the road. Blood in a matted mess of blond, silky hair. Blood on the lips of James's dead mother. Blood floating like a small red river above Brendan Brooks's motionless eyes.

Blood on Craig Mitchell's meaty hands.

I had promised not to think about it, promised to keep quiet.

I had promised, with the weight of my heart behind me, to let James do what needed to be done.

I promised.

I lied.

I had been watching him—searching behind the window glass of passing cars to see if Craig's overlarge face would appear there. I could remember every ugly thing he'd ever said. I remembered the look in his eyes and the sucking smack of tongue against teeth, the way the spittle had flecked on the fat pink shelf of his lower lip. Licking his chops at other people's pain. I stood just behind the swinging doors to the kitchen, watching him sit at the bar, watching him swearing and laughing and brazenly drinking beer while he waited for Lindsay to finish her shift and come sit beside him.

I watched the way he watched her, all slow-moving tongue and small eyes, appraising her body as though it belonged to him.

I watched him, and when I couldn't watch him, I closed my eyes and imagined him watching her die. In my mind, a hulking figure clapped and chuckled at the spectacle as somebody beat the life out of her. In my mind, sometimes, he was killing her. They appeared together in the dark. She struggled as he held her, and his pudgy fingers left dirty streaks on the white expanse of her delicate throat. Choking her life away, hard fists landing on soft places, raining down on flesh that cracked, split, and bled. Growing weaker as he ground away. His grunts, her fluttering cries. He would tell her she deserved it. He would call her a bitch, and she would weep and beg and bleed. She would die, again and again.

Wine trickled from the bottle; sweat trickled down my back. I liked being drunk: the dulled senses, the thoughts covered by cobwebs, the feeling that my eyeballs could roll independently of each other to look in all directions at once.

The night was so hot. I closed my eyes and let the world spin out.

Later, long after the wild roses had shed their petals and the sky had turned white and cold, long after Craig Mitchell's name had become synonymous with brutality and blood and a crumpled body on hot black asphalt, I would have another chance. I would make another promise. Later, I would step into the wood-paneled witness box in a courtroom and try not to stare into Craig Mitchell's cold, unblinking eyes, and swear to tell the truth.

This time, it was a promise I would keep.

I woke in the dark sometime later, with my head resting heavily in the grass and a fine strand of drool draped cooly along my cheek. When I put my hand to my face, I felt the raised pattern of fine lines where the lawn had served as a pillow. The scent of crushed grass was everywhere. With a groan, I got to my feet and searched for the bottle, brushing my fingers through the grass until they touched the alien smoothness of glass, then pitching it away into the dark. I heard the splash and hollow *thunk* as it landed in the creek bed.

Up the porch steps and through the door, a flickering light drew me toward the living room. My father would be there, spending the night on the sofa, TV on mute and remote in hand. If I found him in the morning, he would avoid looking me in the eye while saying that he'd fallen asleep there by accident. I held my breath and peered in.

The couch was empty.

But *she* was here.

The dead girl: her face stared out from the television screen, the same wide-eyed police sketch that was plastered all over town, accompanied by the serious monotone of an announcer whose haggard appearance could only fly on the local news. I focused, fighting the waves of nausea that had arrived to accompany the throbbing in my head, catching only the last few words.

"Police are asking anyone with information about the identity of this woman to come forward." The announcer, looking appropriately somber, put a special emphasis on the word "anyone." Police are asking *anyone*. A final plea for help. Cast the net wide and pray that someone knows her—they were out of options.

I leaned forward to hear the rest of the newscast, then jumped at an unexpected sound: the bright clinking of glasses, coming from the kitchen. Steeling myself to face my parents—I had come home drunk before, but never like this—I started carefully toward the door, only to stop at the sound of my mother's voice. Heavy, dull, and uneasy.

"—think we should just give her time," she was saying.

My father's voice was tinged with exhaustion as he answered. "She's running out of time. She's always been a procrastinator. I just don't want . . ."

He didn't finish his sentence, and there was a long silence. The sound of liquid sloshing, of a bottle against the table. I leaned against the wall and closed my eyes, trying to keep my breathing deep and even.

My father spoke again. "But you've talked to her?"

"A couple times."

"And?"

A sigh. "Honey, I'm sure she gets it. You've got to remember how hard it is, being in love at that age. Everything feels like the end of the world."

"But she hasn't broken it off."

"She hasn't told me. But who knows? Maybe she wouldn't."

There was a pause. "I just don't want her tied up in any of this mess. She needs to get out of here, Claire. This place isn't the same as it used to be . . . all this ugliness, and that poor girl—"

"Adam."

My eyes flew open at the sharpness in her voice. There was a long pause.

"Is there something going on?"

"Claire, I'm not supposed to—"

"So the answer is yes."

"You know there are things that I'm not allowed to say."

They were quiet again, sipping in the silence, and I was getting ready to step around the door when my mother's voice came again.

"Just tell me one thing. Our daughter—is there something I should know?"

No answer.

"Yes," he said, finally. In his voice, I could hear exhaustion. And something else.

Fear.

"Please," my mother said. "Tell me."

He told her.

About a footprint, trimmed in blood. About a break between the trees. About a hidden path, a littered yard, a place where evil had hidden all summer in plain sight.

Ten minutes later, still undiscovered, I crept upstairs with my heart in my throat and my father's words still ringing in my ears.

They can't wait anymore.

Whoever did this, he knew where he was going.

Whoever did this, he's still here.

CHAPTER 16

*I*n a small town, unexplained tragedy can only go so long
before it grows teeth, sprouts sharp claws, and turns,
snarling, on its own self. Before fragments of gossip become
rumors, and the rumors become suspicions. Before neighbors
start eyeing each other with the mistrustful narrowness
of oft-kicked dogs. Inside the safe shelter of their homes,
husbands and wives draw the blinds tight and turn to each
other, worrying at small bits of information and wondering
who, who among their shrinking circle of trusted friends,
might still know something he isn't telling.

The police had waited until there was no other option,
no other explanation, no other lead to pursue. They had
kept it quiet, repeating as needed that there was little
evidence about the killer, and even less about the girl.

But little was not the same as none.

———•———

They had found just enough to know that he had come, and left, on foot. Had carved a path back through the roadside brush, through the trees, disappearing into the thick of the forest that climbed the hillside and then gave way to poorly maintained fences that bordered sprawling, woodsy backyards. He had stepped in her blood as he left, dipping the chunky tread of his instep into the fast-flooding pool of red, not seeing in the dark that even in death, she had managed one tiny victory against him.

"D'you see this, boys?" said the chief, tapping his finger against a glossy photograph that showed a barely there cut in the brush. "That, right there, that's how he left."

Jack Francis and Stan Murray, shifting nervously from side to side, squinted at the gap. Jack coughed, restless at the thought of a murderer passing through the forest there, only a mile south of the Point, where so many kids—where he, so long ago it seemed like another life—gathered at night to light a fire, to drink cheap beer in the moist dark. Stan, preoccupied by the sensation of his belt buckle digging into his gut and the related, urgent need to pee, jumped into the silence without thinking.

"But that's a deer trail," he blurted. "If you follow it long enough, it goes practically out to the Point."

Stan looked to Jack, who immediately got interested in a small clump of dirt that had settled on the linoleum near his toe. The chief fought against the urge to pity them, to guide them away from the board and into the small kitchen, where he'd pat their shoulders with paternal assurance and tell them not to worry, that he'd handle it, that it would all be fine. Together, the younger men were two kids playing dress-up—holstered and buttoned into uniforms that hung in stiff folds from their not-broad-enough shoulders. They had signed up for traffic stops, for small-town disputes, for the occasional call from a wife whose husband had cracked her across the cheek one time too many. They had expected to get fat on doughnuts and flash their badges for fun at the local bar.

Neither of them, for all their swagger, had signed up to stand face-to-face with the reaper. All summer, Jack had been waking up just before dawn with cold sweat prickling on his temples and soaking the sheets beneath him, remembering the milk-blue glaze of her dead eyes, the skin that draped like parchment on her alabaster bones.

The silence broke when the older man tapped the board again.

"I think we have to face facts: there's no chance, none at all, that our guy found a deer trail, in the dark, by accident."

Stan only blinked, but in Jack's eyes, there was dawning horror.

"He knew it was there."

The chief's nod was slow and deliberate. "Yes. Yes, he did. So the person who did this knows our back roads, and he knows our woods, and that means he knows too much to be anything but a local."

And he did. He knew. He had stepped through the brush and into the dark, disappeared up the hillside, where the thick trees gave way to small homes bordered by the forest. Small, lonely homes where people could come and go in privacy. Homes that were owned by dead old ladies, where the front yard was littered with tossed trash and car parts. Homes that sheltered men who nobody loved, hard-drinking and hard-hitting and willing to hurt.

Men who liked to watch things burn. Men who knew our roads and forests but who weren't, who would never be, one of us.

That night, Jack would have another dream. In it, he walked the familiar streets of his forever-hometown, stepping cautiously around corners, peering up at houses that peered back at him with locked-and-shuttered suspicion. Knowing that in a dark room, behind dark windows, something was pressing its face to the glass and watching him with cold and loveless eyes. And from somewhere, from every direction, faint but growing louder, came the sound of someone sobbing.

When Jack woke up in the dark, he realized it was him.

AMELIA

"*L*uke."

He looked up at her, as expectant as a puppy, and she felt her stomach begin to tie itself into hard, angry knots. This was so unfair. She hated to hurt him, of course, she'd never wanted to hurt him, but even as she pitied him, a cold wall of irritation rose up and enveloped her heart.

"Just say yes," he begged. The skin around his eyes had drawn back and his mouth was curving into something between a smile and a grimace. Already, this wasn't going as he'd hoped.

"Luke, please stand up. Let's talk, okay? Let's talk about it."

They had *never* talked about it, she thought, as her anger began to grow teeth and she asked him again to *stand up*, dammit. They had barely even discussed moving in together—it was all Luke, Luke maneuvering, Luke deciding, Luke just assuming that whatever he wanted, she wanted, because that was how it worked. The future businessman, ruled by logic, pressed and polished and always knowing just how things ought to be.

All the happiness—the relaxed confidence of only a few hours before, the easy smile and gentle teasing—left his face. His features turned rigid, stony. He stood up, straightening his clothes, angrily smoothing away wrinkles and adjusting his glasses. His lips pressed together once, then closed hard and tight.

"Please," she said, "let's talk about this."

"There's nothing to talk about," he said. He brushed past her, brushed against her harder than he needed to, and began to crunch his way back toward the car.

She turned and cried after him, exasperated. "Don't I get to have any say in this?"

He whirled around. "Yeah, you get a say. You can say yes, or you can say no. And obviously, you're saying no. So, fine, let's just go."

He turned again and began to walk away. Anger flooded through her so quickly that red spots bloomed suddenly in her peripheral vision, then faded as she strode forward and grabbed him by the sleeve.

"Luke, there's something I have to tell you."

He drew himself up to his full height and looked down his nose at her. His mouth trembled and she thought, *This. This is how he looks when he doesn't get what he wants.*

"Come on," she said, working hard to keep her voice level. She walked the last few steps to the car and perched on the hood, patting the spot next to her, inviting him to come sit. He didn't move.

"Have it your way," she sighed. "Just listen, okay? I love you." He scoffed at this, but she ignored it and pushed on. "I love you, but I can't marry you. I mean, not just you, anyone. I'm not ready to get married."

He looked down at the ring in his hand, then back at her. The lost-puppy look was back.

"I just want to get engaged," he said. "We don't have to get married right away."

She shook her head, firmly. "It's too much, Luke. I'm flattered that you asked, I really am, but my life—" She broke off, realizing that she still had no idea how to tell him the truth.

His voice cut into her thoughts. "Oh, here we go. I was wondering when you'd do it."

She gaped at him. "What?"

"You think I didn't see the way you looked at me before?" he snapped. "I'm not stupid, you know. You've been biding your time, waiting to break up with me—right? Well, here you go. Perfect timing!"

He whirled and stalked back to the driver's-side door, yanking it open and then staring at her over the top of the car. She sighed, turning back to look at the small lights, far away, warm and friendly. That sweet smell was still creeping around in the air, brushing up against her cheek and teasing her nose, disappearing and then reappearing stronger than before.

A memory came flooding back to her, sudden and

surprising—her mother, stepping in from the garden with dirt on her knees and a flush in her cheeks, beaming with pride as she showed her oldest daughter the bounty she held in her hands, a spray of pink and white flowers with sunny, yellow centers and a fragrance so powerfully sweet that it nearly knocked her flat. Thoughts of her mom had always made her smile, but this one was different; tears pricked her eyes and her heart ached with longing. That smell . . .

"Wild roses," she said, looking back at Luke with surprised eyes, as though he'd asked a question.

"What?" he said, bitterly.

She shook her head, but the scent lingered. It seemed to have worked its way into her clothes, had braided itself into her hair.

"Nothing. Look, Luke," she called after him as be began to duck into the car, "I'm not breaking up with you."

His head reappeared, the bitterness on his face replaced by a confused look.

"What? Then why—"

She patted the spot next to her again.

"Just let me talk, all right? Please?"

Reluctantly, he settled next to her, leaving two feet of angry space between them and then finally, unhappily, moving a few inches toward her when he began to slide off the hood.

She took a deep breath.

"Okay," she said. "I've been accepted to an MFA program. In Boston."

He stared at her. "I don't know what that means."

"It's graduate school." She paused. "For acting."

He kept staring. Encouraged by his silence, she rushed forward, allowing herself to get caught up once more in the excitement, the possibilities, the feeling of joy and accomplishment she'd had ever since she realized what her future might hold.

"It's one of the most prestigious programs in the country, Luke," she said, her eyes shining. "I never would have even thought to try, but Jacob said I should think about applying—that I'm really gifted, that I could have an incredible career. So I did, I applied. And after I auditioned, and I found out that they were going to take me . . . I mean, God, I was just so excited and I didn't know how to tell you, you know? I wasn't sure what you'd say, and it never seemed like the right time. And then things got so strange at the end of the year—"

She broke off, abruptly. Luke's eyes had grown narrower while she spoke, his face morphing into a mask of disgust. His lip curled up in a sneer.

"Luke, why are you looking at me like that?"

"Acting," he said flatly. He stared at her.

"Yes," she said, her voice faltering. The excitement of the previous moment seemed to evaporate from her body and disappear on the wind. She shifted uncomfortably and winced as her skin caught against the hood.

He stood, and to her utter shock, he spat into the dirt.

"Acting," he said again, and shook his head. "You have got to be fucking kidding me."

The car door slammed. She sat, stunned, as she heard

the ignition click, felt the engine turn over. Looking back, she saw Luke, sitting behind the wheel. In the spacious interior of the car, he looked very small and mean.

So this is how he looks, she thought again, *when he doesn't get his way.*

This time, the thought made her shudder.

CHAPTER 17

*I*n the days, months, years that followed, I would lie awake and drive myself crazy, wondering what might have been. I would imagine what things might look like now, if I had had more time to think. If I had worked my shift, all busy hands and racing mind, and allowed passing time to illuminate the possibility that I had made a terrible mistake. If, hearing those heavy footsteps behind me in the alley, I had turned and run without looking back.

In the aftermath, I would never stop wondering what could have happened, if I'd only had a little time.

But before I could do anything, before I could gain clarity or perspective or take a deep breath and think, it was over.

Craig Mitchell found me first.

I was alone in the alley that ran along the side of the restaurant, crouched in a shady place near the wall and disgustedly hosing down a line of wooden crates that reeked of spoiled produce—two full crates of tomatoes, quarts and pecks of peaches and strawberries, the sad outcome of a distracted summer where people were staying indoors. Hangover sweat soaked my underarms and my stomach lurched with every wave of stench; gray clouds were moving in, blotting away the sun, but the heat was still unbroken. In the still air, the scent of decay was everywhere. The fruits had grown slow mold in the cold room, their skins puckering as patches of blue-white fur bloomed on their surfaces.

Inside my head, my thoughts raced ahead and then doubled back, circling the place on the side of the road where a stranger's blood had colored the dirt crimson. James had been stubborn, had refused to believe me when I told him my suspicions, had been so convinced of his friend's inability to do harm that he had almost convinced me, too.

Almost.

But Craig had been there.

And James would have to listen.

The strawberries were going if not gone, enormous and red and heavy. I pressed my finger against one and watched it bleed, giving as though it might collapse in on itself.

Flesh could be crushed so easily.

At the end, nature made things so painfully, impossibly delicate.

With sudden fury, I closed my hand, hard. My nails bit and bruised, the berries squelched between my fingers, juice and pulp and seeds erupting, settling into the half-moon depressions where my fingernails grew.

I didn't want to do this anymore. I didn't want to think. I didn't want to wait for James to come back, whatever my promises. I wanted it to rain, until the lake swelled and rushed again, and the streets turned slick, and the water had pounded away every last shred of the girl on the side of the road. And then, with everything dark and wet and smelling of earth, I wanted to start over.

"Hey," said a voice to my left.

I yelped and jumped from my crouched position, turning, realizing as I did that my eyes were wet and my nose was running. I swiped at both with the hem of my sleeve.

Craig stood by the corner of the building, watching me with narrowed eyes. He had the look of someone who'd been standing a while unobserved: self-satisfied, sneering. Knowing what I did, even the sight of him gave me the creeps; I had abruptly stopped sweating, and the hairs on my neck were standing on end.

"What's up?" I said, struggling to keep my tone even, unconsciously taking a step backward. "Do you . . . need something in the restaurant?"

"No," he said.

Another step back. "Lindsay isn't out here. She's inside."

"I know," he said.

I stared at him. My body was prickling now, every nerve ending leaping and firing and ready to send me running. I was suddenly hyperaware of the drying, sticky mess in my palm. I lifted my hand and wiped it away against the wall.

"So if you wanted to see her . . ." I trailed off, looking at him. Another step back.

His lips curled, teeth in an even row beneath. They were surprisingly white.

"No, *Rebecca*," he said, pronouncing it with a sneer. He mocked me, hands on hips, his voice high and haughty: "I don't need to see her."

My pulse throbbed in my ears. Why was he here?

He won't hurt you, I thought. *There are people here. He won't hurt you.*

"Okay," I replied, raising my voice a little, hoping that someone—Tom—would hear me and come to investigate. "Then why are you here?"

I looked over his shoulder, to the safety of the door, my escape blocked by the sheer bulk of him, then turned cautiously to look behind me. The alley ran behind the building and connected with another, smaller one that led to the street. He was ungainly, out of shape. I could outrun him, if I had to.

"You're a real piece of shit, you know that?" I turned again, alarmed at how close his voice was. He had moved toward me while my back was turned. "Why can't you ever just be polite, huh?"

I stared at him, suddenly gripped by anger, flight instincts replaced by fight, my logical fear drowning the desire to let him have it. To say what I'd always wanted. What could he do? It was as good as done; they knew. They were coming. I lifted my chin and stared him down.

"Craig, it's over."

"What?"

I rushed in. "It's *over*. They know you were there.

Whatever happened, whatever you did . . . they know, and you're running out of time."

For just a minute, the hateful gleam of his narrow eyes flickered with something else.

Uncertainty. Maybe even fear.

"What the fuck do you mean, 'whatever I did'?"

I took a deep breath.

"You know what I'm talking about."

I thought of James, saying, *He didn't mean it.*

It was only a joke.

You don't understand.

"Look," I said, allowing my voice to grow softer, willing myself to meet his eyes, "it doesn't have to be like this. If you leave right now and just tell them the truth about everything—"

He growled and advanced on me. "You think you know everything, don't you."

I gulped and tried to look unafraid. "I know enough."

He moved more quickly than I could have imagined, his hand reaching out to snake across the exposed small of my back and around my waist. I screamed and spun, my heart thudding in my chest, squirming desperately against his grasp. Sour breath filled my nostrils. His face was inches from mine. His thumb dug into my ribs.

In that moment, I knew that I had been wrong. That Craig *would* hurt me, would hurt me no matter who might see him do it, would hurt me because he liked it and because hurting people was what he did.

The hand around my waist tightened. I struggled, but he held tight to me, dipping his face even closer, close enough to kiss me.

"And why do you care so much? Is it because you've got so much in common? Because that dead bitch was just another nosy whore who fucks everything up, just like you?"

"Let go!" I screamed, squirming again—and incredibly, he did, shoving me away from him so abruptly that my shoulder rang painfully against the brick wall. He stared down at me, breathing hard. His fists were clenched into tight balls at his sides, the collar of his shirt soaked through with sweat.

"We were tight until you came along, you know that?" His voice was shot through with bitterness, growing louder. "Everything was great, and then you decided he wasn't good enough!"

"Listen," I said. My mouth moved, forming words, while my eyes registered the now-empty space between me and the door. We had gotten turned around in the scuffle, I had ricocheted off the wall and found myself suddenly closer to safety.

My left foot found purchase against the wall. My right followed it. One slow step back, and another.

"Listen—"

"Like hell, I'll listen!" he shouted. "You've been keeping him at your stupid house all summer long! It's like you've goddamn brainwashed him! Every time I call, it's all, sorry, I'm going to Becca's! Sorry, Becca doesn't feel like coming up tonight! Sorry, I'm going out of town with Becca and her parents! So if you're so fucking great, why don't you tell me something?"

It didn't make sense. It didn't matter. I could get away. Another step.

Flecks of spit had appeared at the corners of Craig's mouth. His face was contorted with anger, eyes narrowed into slits, lips curled up in a sneering snarl.

"Why don't you tell ME something, you fucking bitch—if you know so much about everything? Why don't you tell me something?"

Another step.

"If you're so much better than me, why are you still hanging around this town?"

I stopped. In his anger, he didn't even notice, only balled his fists tighter with rage and howled, blasting me with the question that someone, anyone should have asked.

"If you're so much better, why the fuck are you still here?!"

I turned.

I ran.

They were the last words he ever said to me.

CHAPTER 18

By the time the grease-spattered kitchen clock had wound its slim hands around to point to ten o'clock, my mind had wandered back and forth over the same territory so many times that I no longer had to think. There were well-worn grooves in my memory, paths I could walk blindly and automatically, making effortless leaps over the gaps and landing firm-footed on the other side. There was the dead girl, her eyes open, laughing and alive while a pair of narrow eyes traced with want over the curves of her body. There she was again, tangled hair and skin like rice paper, her eyes glazed milky by death, the awkward pile of her broken limbs blocked out by his bulky shadow.

She had died just as I went to sleep that night, had closed her eyes in tandem with mine.

In a way, we had been twins. I had closed my eyes on the vision of James, sitting in the cab of the truck, driving away in the wordless aftermath of breaking my heart. She had closed her eyes on the tall shadow of a killer, a hulking behemoth in long, heavy shoes, passing silently over her broken body and stepping away into the brush.

Together, I imagined, we had stared into the dark and wondered how everything could go to hell so terribly, irreversibly fast.

And then, she had died. And left me to face this trespasser—the one who had arrived on a cross-country flight, who lived in a dead woman's house, who settled like slow poison over the town—alone.

In the dining room, the last two customers were plodding their way through the final bites of a meal. In the low light, turned down to a dim glow for the benefit of the barflies, they were two shadows punctuated by the white dab of a napkin, the slow silver arc of a fork.

"Ugh, could they be any creepier?"

Lindsay had appeared behind me, her hand cocked irritatedly on her hip. She pointed across the room. There was a group of men at the bar. *The* group, the one from Silver Lake, who'd been arrested with such fanfare and who'd been quietly let out of jail by sundown, when the man they had beaten declined to press charges. We could only guess what the cost of his silence had been.

One of the men was watching me, his small eyes gleaming like deep-set, polished steel, his pebbly teeth set in something like a smile. He leaned in close to the man next to him, muttered something. Both of them turned to look at me.

I stared back, wondering why the one with the pebbly

teeth looked so familiar, then realizing that I'd seen him just hours before. He had been in the parking lot as I fled from Craig; I'd bolted past him, too scared and running too hard to think about how close he'd been standing.

Close enough to hear raised voices from the alley.

Close enough to be staring at me now, with the smug self-assurance of a man who thought he knew a secret.

"I can't believe Tom lets them hang out in here," she sniffed. "After what they did. That's probably why Craig hasn't come tonight. He hates those assholes just as much as I do."

"Is he supposed to be here?" I asked cautiously.

She sighed. "I don't know. I guess . . . Tom kinda asked him not to come around. Said he was bad for business."

I nodded.

"But he's not really so bad," she said, her voice almost pleading.

"Lindsay . . ."

"He just acts like a jerk 'cause he likes the attention."

Maybe, I thought. Or maybe he liked the idea of her. A woman, helpless and forced to her knees in the dirt, pinned to the ground by a man who took what he wanted and then took more, took everything.

This was what happened to girls who make plans.

"Lindsay, I think there's something you should know."

She looked at me, her expression a mix of confusion and suspicion. Across the room, the men at the bar were listening to our conversation with too much interest.

"Come here," I said.

I grabbed her hand, dragging her back through the kitchen and out the door. As we stepped into the dark, gooseflesh broke out on my skin. The air was clammy—damp, heavy with the scent of earth and the threat of a storm.

"Wow!" Lindsay was saying, twirling in the orange glow of the streetlight so that her hair flew out behind her and her dress ballooned with caught air. She spread her arms wide. "I think a storm's coming! Doesn't it feel like it?"

"Listen." I leaned back against the side of the building, feeling the rough ridge of brick on my back. It grabbed eagerly at the thin cotton of my shirt. A breeze had sprung up from the west, lifting the hem of Lindsay's dress and winding its soft fingers into my hair, playing coyly with the tendrils that lay loose and damp against my neck.

It was going to rain.

Lindsay peered into the dark, her eyes suddenly lit with friendly focus.

I smiled back at her, then realized that her gaze had settled behind me. I turned.

Someone was standing in the shadows between the trees.

Someone tall and broad-shouldered, wearing heavy boots.

Somewhere far away, a door banged. The sour smell of old beer wafted into the night. There was a shout, and then another. The katydids sang louder.

And under the trees, in the sick orange glow of the streetlight, Craig Mitchell stepped forward and smiled.

AMELIA

He was driving angry, taking the turns too tight, overcompensating on the straightaways and allowing the car to meander from one lane to the other. The roads were empty—they had seen no one, not a single other car—but each time he swerved into the other lane, she gripped the door handle tighter and double-checked her seat belt. Beyond the fogged windows, countryside flashed by in swathes, blurs of green and white and black that she tried to follow with her eyes—trying to count the seconds, to see if she was right to be worried that the car was moving dangerously fast.

Luke had been silent, furious and stone-faced. He wouldn't speak, only glared at her, until she felt afraid to move. The air in the car was full of invisible knives, all pointing at her, all ready to cut.

"Luke," she said, for the fourth—fifth?—time. "If you'd just talk to me—"

"I don't see what there is to discuss," he snapped. His voice was taut and angry, but she sighed with relief anyway. He was talking, at least. Anything was better than the barbed silence.

"Well, *us*, for one," she said. He eased off the accelerator, and she relaxed. Under her nervousness, there was still the sense of endless patience. Whatever he could dish out, she would be fine—she understood him, after all, and this wasn't really about her. He was scared.

And maybe, she thought, I just don't care.

There had been a time when she might have—early on, when she knew less about Luke's moods and believed that every snappish moment must be somehow her fault, she had been hurt by his willingness to lash out. To take his stress and irritation out on whatever, or whoever, happened to be closest, especially when the closest thing was so often *her*. But then, as the months had passed, she had come to see it as something else. A cycle. Unstoppable, like the seasons, like the tides. Luke's snappishness had no cause; like the weather turning cold or the slow decay of fallen leaves, it just happened.

And so she had stopped caring—or, at least, stopped worrying over it. Had stopped investing herself, had stopped trying to fix it, had simply stepped aside and waited for the storm to pass. But as he glared at her and struggled to speak, she found herself thinking that things had changed. Only a little. She had seen something better and bolder, had taken a step down an untested road and found something beautiful waiting for her. Luke, still on his own unquestioned track, seemed further away than he ever had before. She felt the sense of distance, felt that she was looking at him from a different perspective.

Tolerance might not be enough, she thought. Not anymore. He was being left behind. And he knew it.

"What do you want to talk about 'us' for," he snapped, biting the words off as though each one was a punch to the gut. "I think you've talked enough for both of us, right? Just going off and applying to some . . . some ridiculous shit in Boston, without even telling me?!"

"I didn't think you'd understand," she said quietly. "And it seemed stupid to try, when I never thought I would get in. If Jacob—"

He cut her off.

"Didn't think I'd understand?" he yelled. "I've been nothing but understanding! Jesus Christ, Amelia! You go off and drop your freaking classes, load up on all that crazy stuff taught by people nobody has ever even *heard* of, and then you start hanging around with those people all the time—"

"*Those people?*"

"—and I was nothing *but* supportive of you! I let you go off and do whatever the hell you wanted! Even when you started to change, I never said a godda—"

"Started to change?" she shouted, her voice so loud that the windows seemed to rattle.

Luke's mouth dropped open, the rest of the words he'd intended to fling at her lost in the face of her anger.

She took a deep breath and looked out the window, watching the countryside pass, the yellow flash of a mile marker. She waited until it had disappeared, fading into the darkness behind them, before turning back.

"Wow, Luke. You really don't understand me at all, do you," she said.

It wasn't a question.

She forced herself not to scream, looking back out the window instead as she said, "Don't you get it? If I changed, it's because I found something that matters to me. This is my life, don't you see that? Before I found this—before the stage, before Jacob showed me that I had this inside of me—it was like nothing was real. I was just floating with the tide, doing what I was supposed to do, doing what everyone expected of me, because there was *nothing else.* Nothing that lit me up, nothing that made me feel alive like this. I thought you'd be happy for me!"

He scoffed. "So I was just something you were supposed to do, is that it?"

"No, Luke," she said evenly. "I loved you." She paused, realizing that she had used the past tense. He didn't seem to notice. She cleared her throat. "You know I care about you. But I can't be counting on another person to create a life for me. I have to do that, I have to find what makes me happy and do it, and this . . ."

"It's a pipe dream," he snapped.

Incredibly, she laughed. Lightly, like she was genuinely amused, like she had just never realized how funny he really was.

"Now you're joking," she said. He glared back at her, and she returned the look with a smile. "This is a serious program, for serious people. The fact that I got in, it means . . . Christ, do you think I'd commit to something like this if I didn't think it was real? If I didn't have anything less than a great chance of making it happen?" She shook her head, and began laughing even harder. "I majored in business! Business!"

He pushed the accelerator to the floor again, furious in the face of her flippancy, and the motor roared. Feeling the surge of the car as it began to speed, fifty miles per hour, then sixty, then seventy, she swallowed her laughter and turned back to him with her mouth set in a grim line.

"I love you, Luke," she said. "I do. But I won't give this up."

Minutes passed. Outside, the darkened countryside flew past them, the stars becoming a blur overhead. She stopped waiting for an answer, cracked the window and listened as the wind howled its way in, drawing her hair away from her neck and making it dance in the slipstream overhead. The car barreled between a copse of trees, faster now, around a long curve and met with the merging Y of a new road. A green rectangular sign that read 128 flashed momentarily in the darkness and then was lost behind them. The trees overhead thinned, then disappeared entirely, giving way to a wide-open blackness that must be a field. The harsh whipping of the tall grasses that lined the road rose and fell, like urgent whispers.

She opened the window farther, pressed her face into

the gaping space, opening her mouth to taste the air and wondering whether she should just ask him to pull over now, to let her out. She could find her own way back, and anything was better than this—the car full of angry silence, bitterness sitting thickly between them, Luke's infuriating inability to see her as anything but a vessel for his own banal dreams of a yuppie future.

"I can't help noticing that you keep mentioning Jacob."

She lifted her head away from the window and looked at him carefully.

His voice was different, hollower, with none of the previous whining petulance of a scorned little boy. He took another turn too fast, and the wheel touched dangerously close to the grit that lay at the roadside, spinning briefly before finding purchase again on the asphalt.

"Luke, please slow down."

"Don't try to change the subject," he said, and pressed the accelerator harder. "I can't believe I never noticed it before. So obvious, right? I mean, you and Jacob—"

"What? That's ridiculous! He's my professor!"

"I didn't call any of my professors by their first names," he sneered.

She stared at him.

"But maybe I should have," he said, and the cruelty in his voice shocked her. "Maybe if I did, I'd be on my way to some sort of *masters* program instead of an entry-level job pushing papers, right?"

"You're being disgusting," she spat. "You know better than that."

"Oh, I don't know, _Amelia_," he retorted, and the snide tone began to drip with ugly bitterness, and she wondered how she could have missed this. This petty, sneering, self-involved brat, who she had thought—had actually thought!—could be part of her future. He was looking at her.

He was looking at her too long.

"Luke, please watch the road."

"What, you're not going to answer my question?"

He was toying with her now. The motor roared louder as he pushed the pedal harder, watching her get scared, _liking_ how she looked with worry and fear painted so openly across her face.

"Luke—"

"C'mon, why don't you tell me? Just tell me! What've you got to hide?"

"Luke, please—"

"Is that why you like it rough now, huh? Is that how _he_ likes it?"

Her voice was growing panicked now, and she looked frantically down the road, and her hands began to shake, and—

"Luke, _please_—OH MY GOD!"

He looked up and his eyes widened.

Ahead, so close, too close, were two copper-colored disks. The blazing eyes of a tawny doe, a four-legged ghost standing dead center in the road.

He wrenched the wheel, and the tires squealed, and the road disappeared behind them as the car veered into the yawning blackness.

CHAPTER 19

Years later, after so many retellings, there would come a time when any rhythm or flow to what happened that night was lost forever. The story, if there ever was one, was gone. Each moment seems to exist alone now, a snapshot full of shadows and bare knuckles and bared teeth, all of it washed over by the dull, orange streetlight glow that painted the whole world in a flat and lifeless shade of sick.

There is no narrative now, no "And then," only a disjointed series of images. A pile of photographs I've flipped through so many times that I don't even need to look at them anymore to know what's there, to see it, to cover my face with my hands and cry.

There is Craig, stepping into the street, lit from above with lurching, shifting shadows playing under his nose and in his mouth.

There is Lindsay, looking back at me, the smile falling from her face and slinking away into the dark.

There is the song of the katydids, the rush of the wind, the small thud of moths committing slow suicide against the streetlight's hypnotic orange bulb.

There are the men from Silver Lake, sure-footed despite the sour smell of alcohol on their breath, frozen in time beside the open door.

Their mouths are open.

The air is clammy.

Everywhere, people are shouting.

Craig called out and Lindsay moved, the angles of her body shifting, as though she wanted to go to him. I grabbed her arm.

"Don't."

He shouted, louder, "Lindsay!"

"Don't," I said again, urgency coloring my words red. She stared at me, confusion painting itself in lines between her eyebrows and at the corner of her mouth.

Every sound was sharp, barking, biting. The front door of the restaurant banged open again, and two more men spilled onto the street. Their too-loud voices ripped through the night as they spotted Craig. The men advanced in lockstep, like soldiers, smelling of whiskey. One of them pointed at Craig and called out angrily, a shout that was more noise than words.

In the sky overhead, the clouds had moved in low and fast, laced inside and underneath with the threatless flash of heat lightning. It burst in flickering threes, muted by the clouds. The leaves on the trees turned their blanched white bellies toward the wind. Rustling. Whispering. Sighing harshly as their dry bodies brushed together.

Lindsay had turned to look at me, her eyes searching my face for answers.

"Becca," she started, and I looked over her shoulder to the place where Craig stood, heard the deliberate tread of his heavy shoes.

"Lindsay," I said, and grabbed her by the wrist, to hold her there. My voice broke. "Lindsay, it's *him*."

I turned and pulled, feeling her tendons sliding under the thin skin of her forearm, trying to drag her back to the safe light and familiar sounds of the kitchen. She looked at me and then back at Craig, not understanding, seeing my fear but not knowing where it came from or why. She wrenched her wrist away.

"What are you talking about?" she shrieked back.

The words spilled out of me and winged away into the night.

"He was there!" I screamed. "He killed her!"

Lindsay looked at me as though I'd slapped her. She backed away from me, then turned to look at Craig.

And backed away from him.

"The police found his footprints, they found his tracks! And he's been hiding it and lying to everyone all summer because he was there!"

Craig's face was contorted with rage.

"LINDSAY!" he roared. "She's out of her fucking mind! Come here, NOW!"

She turned to look at him with her eyes wide and her mouth trembling.

He glared back, breathing hard, his eyes full of hate and fear, the orange light washing over his face and glinting off the slimy fronts of his teeth. He took a step toward us.

The rock hit him in the face.

Craig yelped as it ricocheted away into the dark, where it hit and skittered drily against the ground. A dark spot, growing vertically as blood began to trickle down, had appeared on his forehead. My eyes traced an arc back to the hand of the tall man, the one with the small teeth and broken nose, still extended with its fingers splayed open in release.

One of them, not the rock thrower, a different, shorter shadow man with hard muscles and squat legs, said, "So."

"You don't want to do this," Craig said, but the color drained from his face. He took a step backward.

"Of course we do," the man slurred.

And they descended upon him.

The snapshots are disjointed, now, some of them out of order and some only half lit. The dark is full of movement, the staggering ballet of five men with whiskey in their veins and a score to settle, flailing arms and feet that windmill and rise and fall against the shadow on the ground.

There is Craig, with blood in his mouth, fighting.

There is Craig, with blood running from his nose, falling.

He's big, powerful, built thickly and with heavy fists, but he is no match for ten hands and ten feet of righteous rage.

There is Lindsay, screaming.

Their blows landed everywhere, forcing Craig back against the car and then onto the ground, shouting. Screaming. Falling silent as he ducked his head between his arms and curled awkwardly on the asphalt. Every movement seemed to originate from the blur of hulking shadows and end somewhere on the prone body of the man on the ground. One of the standing group, less adept than the others, hung back and began to scream, his voice high-pitched and spiraling out of control.

"Tell us what you did! Tell us! Tell us what you did!"

Lindsay ran toward them, shouting something, begging them to stop, stop. Her outstretched hands looked like claws. One of the men caught her and pushed her back. She stumbled and fell to the ground, landing heavily on her knee on the unforgiving road. When she stood up, I could see blood and asphalt.

There is blood on the road.

The air is full of shouting.

Craig had stopped fighting back, had stopped recoiling from the blows that rained down on his heavy body, had gone limp and lifeless. The only sounds came from the men around him, the dull smack of fists on flesh, the asthmatic wheeze of one of the attackers as he sucked in air between punches, the scuff and strike of feet against the pavement. And in the trees, the raucous singsong of the katydids.

Lindsay, her face a slick mess of snot and tears, pushed past me and disappeared, screaming, into the restaurant.

I stayed. My legs had never felt so heavy. They were

paralyzed, immovable. They weighed hundreds of pounds.

The hitting went on for minutes, hours, went on forever, until it stopped. Each man stood aside, one by one, shoulders rising and falling in tandem with the bulging, heaving shadows on the ground. Darker than the shadows, creeping in all directions, was blood. It poured out of Craig's face, out of the place where his face should have been, where I could make out only the mottled hole of his mouth in a mass of wet meat. Air whistled through it, guttural, ragged. One of his teeth was on the ground.

One of the men turned his head away and said, "Oh, shit."

Another sat heavily and all at once, collapsing gracelessly to the ground.

The lightning flashed again, rolling through the clouds, as everyone's eyes rolled toward the sky. The brittle scratch of dry leaves came again; the wind lifted my hair from my neck. It moaned in my ears. The dull orange light brightened and then flickered, the shadows jumped and deepened. One of the men walked unsteadily toward the line of parked cars, two halting steps and then three quick ones, bent double, and vomited. It hit the ground like water.

Blood and vomit on the road.

Behind me, a door slammed. Somebody—Tom, I thought—said, "Oh, God."

And then, slowly, the sick orange night was filled with color. Strobing reds and yellows that played like flickering Christmas on the trunks of the trees and the bare brick face of the bistro building, whites and reds and yellows that bathed us all in light. Ambulance. Police. People clustered and wandered in the street, some running, some shouting, two carrying a stretcher and two others flinging open the ambulance doors.

The chief, his shiny pate slicked with sweat, gave me a long look over someone else's blood-spattered shoulder and then turned away.

Craig was on the stretcher, two men staggering with the weight of him, now joined by two more. He disappeared inside the ambulance. Lindsay was there, her face a mask of misery. She stood by her car, keys in hand, shifting awkwardly from one foot to the other as the doors closed and the siren sounded a mournful note. When they pulled away, I stepped forward and reached for her.

"Don't fucking touch me," she hissed.

"Linds—"

"DON'T!" she screamed, shoving me back. I stared at her, dumbly, while she slammed her car door and twisted the key in the ignition. Her eyes met mine; her lips were moving. When she pulled away, her tires left brief, dark tracks made of Craig's blood.

In my head, I could still hear her voice—so quiet, but as smooth and clean as ice above the purr of the motor.

"You stupid bitch," she'd said. "Don't you get it?"

Don't you get it?

You do not.

Fucking.

Belong here.

CHAPTER 20

*I*t is, after all, these small-town tragedies that truly bring a community closer together. That separate the outsiders from the ones who belong. That keep the gates closed, and the doors locked, and the evil of the wider world safely outside.

We don't trust you if we don't know you, and sometimes, we don't trust you if we do. We band together; we circle the wagons; we peer out of our shuttered windows with weapons in hand and loved ones at our side.

When the blinds are drawn and the stakes are high, only the lucky few are allowed to come in.

Brendan Brooks had been cold in the ground when the questions finally came. Long after the body was pulled from the water in the faint, low glow of the setting sun; long after the somber Chief of Police had sat in an air-conditioned living room, a cup of coffee growing cold between his weather-worn hands, and tried his best to offer comfort; long after two parents had sobbed themselves into a fitful sleep where the words "massive head trauma" and "died instantly" echoed like schoolyard taunts. It was weeks later, with the scrim of exhaustion draped heavy over their bloodshot eyes, that Bob and Linda Brooks asked why nobody had warned them about the monstrous metal beast beneath the surface of the lake.

"Those boys," Linda said, her voice high and wet with choked-back sobs, "they could have warned him. They were right there. Why didn't they warn him?"

The last sentence a scream.

"Why didn't you tell us?!"

Those she asked could only stare, and stutter, and turn away.

How could we explain? That nobody had been told because nobody had ever needed to be told; that to the minds of the boys at the bridge that day, the inviting pool below may as well not have existed; that without knowing why, they knew that on that side of the south shore bridge, you do not jump.

That those who live here knew—had always known—that a red Ford tractor with a long-armed front-end loader was hidden in the water at the south end of Silver Lake.

It was late in the summer when Linda Brooks came back. Alone and with a bare, pale band of skin on her left hand, in the place where her wedding ring had been. She moved back into the little house by the lake, spending her nights in the wood-paneled bedroom whose window now looked out on the place where her only child had died. Days, she could be found in town—pushing an empty shopping cart slowly up and down the aisles of the grocery, dragging her limp fingers over the fat jars of jam and store-brand canned peas in their even rows, fixing her red-shot glare on the shoppers who dared, as her son lay cold in the ground, to keep on as though nothing had happened.

The store became a tomb. People had always gathered at the butcher counter or around the long, gray refrigerator case lined with cold beer, filling the place with a low hum of chatter that rose and fell with the ringing of the register. But nobody could do that now—not with Linda Brooks pacing her grief up and down the aisles, her hollow eyes full of directionless accusations, blame for every single one of us, the thoughtless secret keepers who let her son die. Instead, the grocery stood empty, occupied only intermittently by furtive people who slipped in and out with their purchases as quickly as possible and who fled, at the sound of the mourning woman's slow footsteps, to hide behind the produce. We ate every leftover in the fridge, ate canned beans and instant rice from our pantries, ate gas station crackers smothered in E-Z CHEEZ rather than risk encountering that stare, those steps, the plaintive whine of the cart's wheels singing emptily down the fluorescent aisles. And as the cupboards grew bare, the tension grew thicker.

"Something has to be done," people said.

"It can't go on like this," they said.

Until the evening in August, with the twilight deepening on the lake and the crickets singing in the brush, when three women drove over the bridge, past the watchful eyes of the entry guard, and through the southern gate of Silver Lake. They parked an ancient Jeep at the cracked mouth of the driveway where, just weeks before, Brendan Brooks had crossed the threshold. Where, for a few strange hours on a hot summer afternoon, the gap between moneyed visitor and resentful townie had ceased to exist. They walked up the shadowed drive with deliberate steps. Two wore nervous smiles; one held a pie.

And for once, no matter how much or who you ask, there is nobody in Bridgeton who will tell you what happened that night. Nobody will profess to having been there; nobody will claim to know someone who knows, for certain and without a doubt, the words that passed between the three women on the porch and the shadowy figure inside, as they stood on either side of a closed screen door. Nobody gossips quietly about what happened when the door opened, and the Jeep remained, and a dim, golden light shone from the living-room window for the first time in weeks and weeks.

In a small town, in our finer moments, we keep our secrets well.

The next day, the furtive few who dared to brave the grocery found it changed. No lurking shadow by the door, no slow squeal of the shopping cart, no mourning zombie to dare you, with her silent stare, to meet her eyes without choking on your own guilt.

The next night, the Jeep was back; the burning lamp, too, and another beside it. On the lawn of the little house, a golden square of light revealed four shadows, huddled close, barely bobbing with the rhythm of long-awaited conversation.

And when winter came, the light was gone, and so was Linda Brooks.

But you can find her here. In town, among us, another winter weatherer with drugstore highlights and a four-wheel-drive truck. In a tidy bungalow, on a quiet street, with a well-kept garden and an oak tree in the yard. You can see her in the market on Sundays, moving quickly, plucking items from the shelves and joking with the cashier, as they both pretend no memory of that terrible summer. You can see her smiling, with sad and shining eyes, at the young men—the four strapping sons of three brave women—who show up each winter to shovel her driveway, and mow her lawn twice a month when it's warm.

And if you ask us, if you ask anyone, she's always been here. Even though it's clear, from her tailored jackets and silky voice and the unsullied glow of her rich woman's skin, that her life was once lived elsewhere. Because she is a good woman, a fine woman. She has strong hands, a quick mind, a generous nature. In the summer, her rosebushes are heavy with blossoms, flourishing and fragrant like no others in the neighborhood; in the winter, her house is warm with the scent of cinnamon and nutmeg. And in her short time here, she's given without measure. Cuttings from her garden. A recipe for lemon tarts, passed down and closely guarded, going back three generations. An open ear, a listening heart, from someone who knows what it is to grieve.

A boy, with an easy grin and gentle nature, lost forever on the cusp of manhood.

Bridgeton claims her as its own, for what she gives us. For what she gave.

For what we took from her.

We cannot give her son back, but we can give her what small towns give best: a fence to chat over. A seat at the bar. A hundred hands to hold in times of trouble; a hundred hearts to share in life's small joys. And one day, when it's time, a patch of sweet, green quiet in the ancient graveyard, where bones both old and new are all at peace beneath the rustling grass.

A place to live, and die, knowing that you were truly home.

AMELIA

The deer crashed away into the brush as the engine *tick-tick-ticked* and then slowed, and died. Terrified into silence, they both watched the bobbing white of her tail as it vanished through a cut between the bushes and into the dark.

When Amelia spoke, her voice was cold and thick with fury.

"What the hell is the matter with you?"

Luke, his bravado cracked, answered her in a tiny, terrified squeak that would have been funny if not for the still-too-close memory of his baseless accusations, the suggestion that she'd slept her way to the top.

"Hang on," he whispered.

He turned the key in the ignition. There was a cough, and then, incredibly, the purr of the motor.

"Okay," he muttered. "Okay."

"Okay?" she snapped, exasperated. "We're in a freaking *cornfield*."

Ahead of them, a long dirt track wound away through the tall green architecture of the cornstalks, many still heavy with green-husked ears that grew out at angles, a soft tuft of silk waving at the end like a tiny flag. In the dark, they looked like skeletons, clustered together uncertainly and whispering over the alien machine that had appeared at the edge of their field. When the breeze blew lightly down the rows, they brushed against each other with a sound like paper.

It gave her the creeps.

Luke ignored her, throwing the car into reverse and backing away.

Amazing, she thought, realizing how close they had come to ruining somebody's crop.

Instead, he had veered right onto the dirt path and clipped only two stalks, which lay like fallen soldiers among their still-standing brethren. She watched the line recede—they waved in the wind, *good-bye*—and then they were on the side of the road.

Luke put the car in park and turned to her.

"Look," he said. For a moment, she thought with relief that he might apologize. Her stomach tied itself into a tight knot when she saw that the cold, cruel look had come back into his face.

"I don't—" she began, and he held up a finger. *Shh.*

"Just tell me the truth," he said. "You fucked him, right?"

Shocked, she could only stare.

"C'mon," he said, his voice louder. "Just tell me the truth. You *fucked him*."

Recovering, she leveled her gaze at him and did not blink. In a voice dripping with contempt, she said, "You know I didn't."

He scoffed, and she raised her voice. "You're pathetic, you know that? It didn't have to be like this! All you had to do was bend the tiniest bit, just give up your precious, precious plan—"

"Oh, that's rich," he snapped. "My plan was fine, until that asshole made you think I wasn't good enough—but you had to be special, right? You had to be a *star*. How many other girls do you think he's told that to, just to get in their pants?"

Her mouth dropped open. He'd scored a point there, he thought, and began to shout at her.

"Why don't you just admit that you did it, huh? You fucked him! C'mon, Ame, why not admit it? Why the big secret?!"

She was quiet for a minute, her lips still parted and the look of disbelief still painted on her face. She began to shake her head, slowly, then crossed her arms and sighed, turning away, refusing to look at him.

"I'm not doing this with you anymore, Luke," she said, quietly. "You won't believe me anyway."

He sat back, mimicking her, crossing his arms and allowing his smile to become smug.

"Yeah, I knew it. I've got you pegged, haven't I? I knew you couldn't do it by yourself."

"What the hell are you talking about?" she snapped.

"All that talk," he said. "All those things you said, wanting to do it all different. Wanting to talk dirty. Look, I'm just saying, I knew it."

She stared at him. His eyes were glazed, glassy, blazing with triumph behind his glasses, and as his lip curled in a sneer, she felt it happen.

Her love for him—whatever shred of it was left—was gone. It had slunk away into the night. It would die out there, and she would not be sorry to leave it, at the side of the road, in a no-name town surrounded by nothing but blackness.

Quietly, she said, "Knew what, exactly?"

He licked his lips.

"I knew you'd never turn into such a whore without a little help."

"Good-bye."

The word was out, and she was gone. Out of the car in a flash of fabric and tossed blond hair, gone so quickly that he barely had time to react. He flung open his own door and looked wildly around—she had run to the back, was trying to open the trunk, and he rushed at her while the vast night yawned away in all directions. There was only the car, the slap of his feet on the pavement, the slim yellow lines that ran unassumingly along the road and disappeared evenly into the distance. And her.

Her.

She saw him coming and moved away, past the hood and into the twin beams of the headlights, and turned under the dizzying canopy of stars with her mouth wide open and her eyes squeezed down to tiny slits.

"It's over!" she screamed, and he could only stare. He stumbled, feeling dizzy, feeling drunk with jealousy and rage.

He clutched at the door as she turned away, walking with her head held high. Hot tears appeared at the corners of his eyes and he swiped them away, hating them, hating his impotence in the face of her anger.

It's over.

He could not make her stop.

Could not keep her.

Could not make her stay.

CHAPTER 21

A raindrop, early and alone in the face of the coming storm, fell from the sky and punched against my temple. It exploded, slithered and slipped through the loose hair near my ear, disappeared under the curve of my jaw.

I was alone.

I hadn't moved for five minutes, then ten, then fifteen, as the wind began to blow harder and the dark puddle of Craig's blood stopped seeping and sneaking away in rivulets on the asphalt. Without touching it, I knew that it had turned sticky, knew that it was drying against the heat of the road just as the dead girl's had done so many days before. When she had bled. When she had died.

Inside the restaurant, shadows moved along the wall and behind the bar, frenetic waves of dark and light as the men inside made some attempt to tell their story. Led inside and with the door locked behind them, I imagined them stumbling backward through the past while the police listened and shook their heads, while the silver circlets of handcuffs bit deeper into their wrists, until they reached the beginning. Before the first kick, before the first punch, before the rock had glanced off Craig's broad shoulder, when the air had been full of shouting and the smell of alcohol and . . . me.

The sound of raised voices drifted across the street—I caught only fragments, the word "murdered," a barked order to be quiet—and I crouched lower in the shadow of the car. A face appeared at the window, unrecognizable behind the wavy glass and scanning the shadow line of the trees. They were looking for me now.

I straightened my legs slowly and then darted across the asphalt, into the alley. Overhead, the sound of tapping: the moths had begun to turn maniacal circles, throwing themselves harder against the orange bulb of the streetlight and then drifting away, carried by the wind.

My mind, gone blank and black in the moments that followed the fight, began to fill with fragmented thoughts. I closed my eyes; the sight of Craig's kicked-in face and broken teeth reared up in the blackness and I felt my stomach twist.

I had to get out of here.

I had to find James.

Together, we would explain everything to the people who needed to hear it.

I was reaching into the pocket of my apron again when I realized that there was no telltale jingle of keys beneath my hand.

Stupid, I thought as shame flooded my face with hot blood. I had come with Lindsay, had allowed her to goad me out and into the role of designated driver, had slipped distractedly into the passenger seat of her car and left my own car at home. Stupid. Stranded.

The thunder came again, closer this time, as the storm barreled over the mountains and into town. Weakened leaves were beginning to loosen themselves from their holdings, tumbling down and along the street in playful loops. The rain was coming, it was getting closer.

Craig would have to confess now, wouldn't be able to run or hide from what—from whatever—he'd done. It was over. They were inside, it was all coming out, the story would be spilling its way down the bar and across the tables and into phone lines that would ring busy with big news. There would be a front-page article, there would be a press briefing, there would be warrants and evidence and confessions in a court of law.

A storm was coming, and the blood in the road would be washed away.

And then, I thought, people would begin rewriting history to show how very unlike us Craig Mitchell had always been.

Closing my eyes, I pulled the cool air—blessedly cool, tinged with damp and stray raindrops and the electric, ozone smell of a storm—into my lungs. Relief flooded through me from the inside out; I felt it creeping through my veins, escaping like steam from the top of my head. The thudding moths seemed to beat a rhythm against the streetlight, their small bodies tapping in twos that registered inside my head like a mantra, joining the rough cry of the katydids in the trees.

All done.

All done.

I was still standing there, face turned skyward and drinking in the night, when the back door of the restaurant slammed and the final words of a conversation kicked down the alley and reached my ears. I recognized Tom's tired voice, and the gravelly cough of the Chief of Police.

"—see her out here?" the chief was saying

There was the rough sound of flint-strike, the quick suck of air. Tom had lit a cigarette. I hadn't even known he smoked.

"Only when you did," he answered. I heard him exhale. "I didn't see her leave."

It was me they were talking about. I slunk backward, into the shadow of the Dumpster, wrinkling my nose and fighting back the urge to retch as the stench of rot hit my nostrils. All those peaches, tomatoes, baking in the hot sun, had begun to sag and stink inside. It was a terrible smell, rancid, fetid, sour and sweet, carried horribly toward me with every light gust of wind.

The chief was talking again, muttering so that I could only half hear his words before they were lost on the wind.

"—find her," he said, the beginning carried away on another rancid gust of air. "You heard what they said . . ."

Another gust.

I wasn't ready to be found. I wanted no part of what was to come.

CHAPTER 22

The first time we'd made love, I marked the time that passed afterward by counting James's heartbeats. I listened to the thudding in his chest and thought that his heart must be closer to the world than most people's; he was so thin, so wiry, that I could feel it fluttering against his breastplate as easily as if it had been encased in linen. Then, in the aftermath of the first time—my first time, and his, and ours—I lay my head against his chest to feel the beats slow from a furious gallop to a light patter.

"Are you okay?" he'd said.

I sat up, feeling awkward and suddenly, exceptionally naked. I registered dim gratitude that my hair, falling in a cavewoman tangle over my shoulders, was long enough to cover my nipples. You can't talk to someone, I thought, if they can look down midsentence and just see your nipples. Nipples are a conversation stopper.

The look on his face was deepening from care to concern. "Becca—"

"I'm fine. I'm fine . . . Better than fine," I added, smiling in a way that I hoped was self-assured.

"Your face?"

I had to laugh. He had elbowed me in the eye at the very beginning, when it had seemed like there was no place for all of our arms and legs to go—no possible way that two people with all these limbs could lie down together, holding each other hip to hip and lip to lip, and actually arrange them in such a way that nobody would get hurt.

Later, when the awkwardness had passed, he had gathered me back into his arms and pulled me up to his chest, up to the place where the hollow rhythm of his heart seemed to knock, knock, knock its insistent desire to be set free. I laid my head against his chest and listened again to that sound, the hollow drumbeat that told me he was still here, still alive, still with me.

With James, I'd never been unsure. Never anxious over what was to come. Never afraid.

I was afraid now.

I was waiting when the truck pulled in, slipping out of the shadows, wide-eyed and paranoid at the possibility of being seen. I had been sitting in the shadows behind the gas station for what seemed like hours, slapping at the mosquitoes that whined in my ears and tried to drain the blood from my neck, watching the road and willing each car to be his. There had been little traffic. Fifteen minutes before, a police car with its lights strobing had sped past, its driver holding the radio to his mouth, the slumped shapes of two silent men sitting in the shadow of the backseat.

I had called him, praying as I punched the pay phone's keys that I was remembering the number right, praying that he would finally pick up, nearly crying with relief at the sound of his voice in the receiver. He was just getting into town, he told me, and what was going on, and I struggled to keep my voice level as I asked him to pick me up.

He had asked where, and asked nothing else.

Alone in the dark, with nothing to do but wait, my mind had begun to race. Back to the night when everything had changed. I wondered whether she had fought back, at the end, when she realized what was happening. When she realized that she would never get out of this town.

I knew how she felt.

James leaned back in his seat, one hand on the wheel, as I slipped through the passenger door and shut it with a thunk. My heart began to thud in my chest, leaping higher, in my throat now. I thought I might choke on it.

"How long have you been back?" I asked, touching the worn handle of the door. It felt cool. At last, cool. Nothing had felt cool this summer. He didn't answer; I didn't wait for him to.

"We have to talk," I said, looking at him and then losing my nerve, looking down at my lap instead. "Something's happened, James. Something bad."

"Tell me now."

I shook my head. "I don't want to do this here. I need to

get away from here, right now, before somebody sees me."

James looked at me for a long time.

"Okay," he said. "Okay."

We drove without direction, grit kicking under the tires as the canopy of trees closed overhead and the lightning grew brighter. The sky was beginning to spit, raindrops falling in twos and threes until they covered enough space for James to turn on the wipers and flick them away. As we had pulled out of the parking lot, I had reached into the glove compartment, jittery and desperate for cigarettes, when his hand slammed the compartment closed.

"Dammit! Don't do that!"

"You need to talk to me," he said.

"I need to smoke," I said, hearing the whine in my voice and not caring. My hands had begun to shake.

"Becca, if you don't tell me what's going on right now, you may not get a chance to."

I stared at him.

"What do you mean?" I said, my voice growing loud. James looked uncomfortable. More drops plunked against the windshield. In the silence, over the whir of the tires, they sounded like music. In the silence, I knew I had to speak.

"Craig knew something, James. He knew who killed that girl, or . . . or he did it himself." I took a deep breath. "He was there."

We were speeding now, careening around curves, the

wheels of the truck fishtailing dangerously close to the slick
grass at the roadside and the deep ditch beyond. James was
hitting the wheel with the palms of his hands, swearing,
demanding that I tell and then retell what had happened at
the restaurant.

"Oh God," he kept saying, "Oh God. Why? Why
would you do that?" and then, "It's not possible," and then—
angrily, now—"How do you know any of this?!"

Reluctantly, I told him what I had seen in my house—
what I had heard.

"I can't believe this."

I slapped the open palm of my hand against the window.
"How can you not? It makes perfect sense! He wanted to
brag about it, all that posturing was just cover for what
he'd done."

"He's been obsessed, Becca, that doesn't make him a
fucking killer."

"Evidence!" I yelled. "I told you what I heard! Doesn't
that mean anything to you?"

"No," said James, and fell silent.

My ears were burning, rage running like fire through my
veins at James's stubbornness, his blind loyalty to someone
who had never deserved it and who had done unspeakable
things. I felt something made of ice uncoil in my stomach,
stretching its angry neck out and opening its mouth to scream.

"Dammit, James! How can you be so blind to this?
I'm telling you I was there, I heard everything! Jesus,
I confronted him! He was going to hurt me, doesn't that
matter to you?! Or maybe it doesn't! Maybe you're more

like him than I thought, maybe you're just another—"

"ENOUGH!" he roared, swerving right over the yellow line that snaked down the center of the road and then back, losing control, barely regaining it as I sat back in the seat. Stunned. Silent.

He was breathing hard again, gripping the steering wheel with hands laced with stress lines, a white cobweb of tension that cracked across every knuckle. We were driving too fast. The road was growing slick, growing dangerous and dark with every passing minute.

"Dammit, Becca," he finally said, and his voice broke.

I looked at the floor. "I didn't mean that."

James shook his head. "It doesn't matter." A sick smile had begun to play at the corners of his mouth.

"Of course it matters."

James laughed, a harsh, bitter sound. "Not anymore. Not now. And this is my fault, I should have just . . . shit, and now what? He's in the hospital? Which one?"

"I don't know."

Another beat passed in silence. James took another turn too fast. Outside, the starved yellow grasses blurred and waved like brittle ghosts in the glow of the headlights, bending toward the truck and then snapping back like switches. The thunder was rumbling closer, the lightning coming in short, bright bursts.

"Lindsay . . ." He trailed off.

"What?"

"This is going to wreck her."

I thought of Lindsay's face, her narrowed eyes, the hiss

of her voice, and felt my face flush with shame and hurt. I shook my head, shook the memory away.

"It would have happened sooner or later. Their relationship . . . it's all a lie. If he did this, he spent all summer hiding it. All summer."

"What's your point," he said.

"Somebody who could do that . . ."

"People hide things for all kinds of reasons, Becca."

"What does that even mean?"

"I'm telling you," he said, gripping the wheel and staring straight ahead, "that there's a lot you don't know. And whatever you think of Craig, whatever his faults, he's still someone I consider a friend."

"That's not what he seems to think," I retorted, suddenly remembering his anger in the alleyway. "He said that you haven't hung out with him all summer. He said . . ." I paused.

"What?"

"He said you've been ditching him to be with me," I said, slowly. "Except—"

I stopped abruptly, and listened to the whoosh of the tires against the pavement. Listened to the thought that had risen, pulsing white and bright like a silent alarm, inside my own head.

"Except," I said, slowly, "you've been lying to him, haven't you? You haven't been with me. I haven't seen you since . . ."

Since the party, I thought, suddenly. Since July. No wonder I'd felt so lonely, so lost. No wonder he had seemed so far away.

"You . . . you've been somewhere else. And I was a convenient excuse."

I thought of Craig, his face contorted, his voice guttural with rage. *A stuck-up bitch who fucks everything up . . . just like you.*

But James had been keeping secrets from me, too.

He slumped in his seat as I looked at him, his shoulders buckling, the breakneck pace of the truck finally slowing.

"James—"

"Not here," he said. "Wait. We're almost there."

There was a sudden snap, and the truck was rumbling over rough road. Looking out the window, I saw trees— thick, close, branches that reached out like fingers to claw at the window. Below us, a rutted drive, carving a hidden two-track opening back away from the road. Above, a heavy canopy of trees rustled and shushed in the growing wind. The tunnel of green opened far ahead, into blackness, in what I knew was endless, open space.

A space covered with rough grass that would be crushed beneath the truck's tires and die, fragrant and sweet, in the night air. It would clog my nostrils, a scent I would never smell again without remembering his body, his hands, his voice. Without remembering the twist of scratchy flannel on my skin. Without feeling heat, unwanted and shameful and instantaneous, between my legs.

I stared at him, and thought I could feel the first thread of something horrible unraveling between us.

The first thought that I—that all of us—had made a terrible mistake.

CHAPTER 23

For a long time, we didn't speak. I watched the clock, counting seconds, waiting for the numbers to change. Once. Twice. Outside, the wind was growing stronger, the treetops tossing wildly as their delicate spines bent this way, then that. The spitting rain smacked the windshield. One heavy drop. A long silence, and then another, then three more in rapid fire.

I twisted my hands in my lap and spoke without looking at him.

"Craig . . ." I began, then faltered before finding the end of the sentence. "He's an asshole," I finished lamely.

"Yes," James replied. "He can be. But that's how it is, isn't it? People can do things, they can do terrible things, but that doesn't mean they're evil."

"I don't understand."

"Don't you?" he asked.

The air in the car seemed suddenly thick, and too hot. I cracked my window before meeting his eyes.

"If you're talking about yourself, it's not the same thing," I said, quietly.

"But not exactly different, either."

It was James's turn to watch the clock, one hand still gripping the steering wheel, the other rubbing against the hard angles of his face. I watched him pinch the bridge of his nose, push his fingertips over the high curve of his forehead and into the mussed tangle of his hair.

"I knew exactly what I was doing," he said, finally. "I saw a way to hurt you first, on purpose, and I took it."

I snapped my head up so quickly that the tendons in my neck clenched painfully, pulling stiff and tight in the spot just below my ear. He watched me carefully, as though weighing what to say next, then began talking again, faster now.

"You've been thinking this was your fault, too. I know you have. No"—he held up a hand as I began to speak— "don't. I need to say this. This is the part where I talk."

I sat back and stared.

"I knew I was wrecking everything," he said. "But I was angry, and I was scared, and so I hurt you on purpose."

It was quiet again. Even the spitting of the rain had stopped, there was no hard smack of droplets against the windshield. In a faraway corner of my mind, I thought what a shame it would be if the storm had passed us by. If we were left the same as we'd been, in the grip of dust and drought, no better off for all we'd been through.

James cleared his throat, and this time, he took my hand.

"And I'm sorry. You already know that I'm sorry, but I just wanted you to know, also—I wanted you to know, I know better than that. I knew better. My mom . . . she raised me better than that."

My face flushed, and I bit back tears, bit down against the urge to fall into his arms the way I would have done only a few short weeks before. I wanted nothing more than to collapse there, to bury my face in his shirt and close my eyes and allow sleep to overtake me while I breathed in the scents of detergent and sweat and old smoke.

Instead, I forced myself to let go of his hand.

"James, we can talk about this another time. Because if Craig didn't do this . . . we have to go to the police."

He gave me a long look, opened his mouth, hesitated and then said, "There's something—"

His voice was drowned in noise as the sky suddenly lit overhead. A jagged scar of electric white opened across the sky, accompanied at the same time by a terrifying, earsplitting crack of thunder.

Rain or not, the storm had arrived. Around the perimeter of the field, silhouetted against the low sky, the trees waved as though trying to uproot themselves from the ground and shed their leaves into the whirling, screaming wind.

I yelped at the loudness of the sound and looked wide-eyed out the window. "Jesus? Are we okay in here?"

James was still staring at me, motionless and pale in the weak green light from the dashboard.

"James!" I said.

He snapped to attention and peered out into the dark. There was another flash of lightning.

"You're right, we should find a better place," he said. His movements were frantic as he turned the key in the ignition, listened as the engine coughed and then purred, looked once over his shoulder and then threw the truck into gear. I reached for my seat belt as he hit the accelerator.

The truck lurched but didn't move.

"Shit," he said, his voice too loud after so much confessional soft talk. "Shit!"

"Try it again," I said, peering out into the dark. There was another crack and flash, this one even closer. "That looked like it hit somewhere in town."

James pressed the pedal again. We both listened as the wheels spun and did not grip.

"I must have landed in a rut," he growled, unbuckling his seat belt and reaching behind him. When he turned back to me, he had a flashlight in his hand.

"Where are you going?"

"There might be a rock or something I can use for leverage," he said. He jumped down, stepping into the wind. His hair began to toss furiously around his head.

I started to unbuckle my own seat belt. "I'll help you!"

"No," he shouted over the wind. "Stay there! I'll just be a minute!"

The door slammed, and he disappeared. I felt the truck shift, slightly, as he leaned against it, testing to see how stuck we really were. In the dim, ghostly beams of the headlights, I could see the deep, dry furrows that ran haphazardly across the field. A summer without rain had turned this place into a mess of holes. It was amazing that we'd made it this far.

There was a tap at the window—I looked up to see James pointing behind the car, back the way we had come. He held up his index finger—one more second—then disappeared again into the dark.

A minute passed, and then another. I peered at the rearview mirror, catching a brief glimpse of the flashlight as it played over the close line of the forest, watching it sweep and then bob away between the trees. Alone, I couldn't stop my thoughts from running crazily in circles, tracing back from James's confession to the terrible sight of Craig's broken body as they hoisted him into the ambulance.

All for nothing. And the dead girl . . .

I put my head in my hands and moaned. I had been so stupid, so fucking stupid.

I needed a cigarette.

Peering again into the dark—I thought I saw the flashlight briefly, bobbing between the trees—I reached for the catch on the glove compartment. James had always kept cigarettes here, had grinned at me as he opened the glove box and pointed to them, sitting alongside the insurance and registration. "Necessities!" he had said, and I had laughed, and so had he.

I smiled weakly at the memory as I pulled the pack toward me, only to fumble and drop it to the floor when another, enormous thunderclap sounded overhead. Reaching down, feeling in the area near my feet, my fingers finally brushed its slick cardboard face. I grasped it, at the same time looking hopefully into the glove box for matches. Or a lighter. There was something there, I thought, the glint of polished silver just underneath the registration papers.

I closed my hand around the object.

Pulled it from the glove compartment.

Smiled briefly as I realized what it was—*James, this is awfully fancy*—and opened the worn catch to look inside.

I hadn't moved, had frozen in place with my hands clamped tightly in my lap, when James climbed back into the car. A rush of damp wind came behind him, lifting my hair and caressing my neck with soft fingers. He was breathing hard as he slammed the door.

"All right, I think we're good," he said, dropping the flashlight behind his seat. "I found a rock that's big enough and if we just—Becca? Are you okay?"

I shook my head, just barely. The blood that rushed in my ears, the wind howling outside, all seemed to say, *Shhh.*

Shhh, don't tell.

Shhh, keep quiet.

Shhh.

I swallowed hard.

Struggled.

My head had never felt so heavy, my eyes never so unwilling to look into his face.

A face I knew.

A face I loved.

A face I had traced the lines of with my fingers so many times, I knew it as well as my own.

James was staring at me. His eyes traveled down

the length of my neck, across my heaving chest, over my tightly clasped hands and down, down to the floor, where cellophane and smooth cardboard shone whitely between my feet.

"Becca," he said, again. The sound of his voice made my hair stand on end.

I forced myself to look up, to look at him, to look into the face of the boy I had loved and trusted and *believed*. All summer long. In my lap, my hands fell open as though of their own accord.

Staring up, immediately recognizable in the dark, was a face.

The wide gray eyes and frozen smile of Amelia Anne Richardson.

I took a deep breath, and everything inside of me fell through the floor.

"It was you."

AMELIA

*B*eyond the glow of the headlights, the night turned terrifyingly dark. There was no moon, no convenient streetlight, no soft electric glow from a nearby house to guide her. She felt the breeze on her face and wondered, as her heart slowed and the blood stopped rushing like an ocean of anger in her head, which way she could go that would lead her to safety. The sky yawned above, cavernous, full of glittering stars that were so, so far away.

Some of them are already dead, she thought, and the idea made her giddy with terror and amazement.

Behind her, Luke was shouting her name. Begging her to come back.

She thought she heard the word *sorry* more than once.

She took another step and tried to imagine a world in which "sorry" could possibly fix this. One where she would forgive him—in which she could go back, accept his apology, forget all the ugly, ugly things he had said. Tried to imagine something, anything, that he could say to undo the damage and make that shred of love come crawling back out of the darkness. If he shouted after her that he was dying. That he had a brain tumor. That he had split personality disorder, that it hadn't been him who said those terrible things, that his evil alter ego who had a ridiculous name like Chaz and also liked to eat mayonnaise straight out of the jar was responsible for everything that had just happened, so wouldn't she please come back.

She took another step. And another. And then, out of nowhere, she felt laughter bubble up inside of her.

Not even then, she thought. Not even then. She was *done*.

There was too much out there, too many beautiful things to see, and she could only be glad that she had found out now—before Boston, before she'd suggested a long-distance relationship or, even crazier, that he come to live with her there. Now, she knew.

Every step away from him felt like a triumph.

Slowing her pace, she stared into the dark, willing her eyes to adjust, praying that a beacon would appear somewhere—a porch light, a television. Another car, piloted by people who would take pity, take her in, take her to a phone where she could call . . . someone.

Luke was still yelling.

She took another step.

She wasn't alone. There were a hundred sounds and smells out there in the dark, she realized, raising her face to the gentle breeze that blew down the road and sniffing at the air. There was soil, and the sweet scent of crushed grass, and the light, festering smell of something decaying—a deer, maybe, down the road and dead in the dirt, its back snapped in two and its eyes eaten away by marauding crows. There was a harsh, gritty sound in the trees, a three- and four-note call and response that sounded like insects, scolding each other. There was singing, too, the sound of crickets in the brush.

And then, she saw it. Off to the right, through the trees—

But no, it was gone. It had been there only a moment, she was no longer sure it had been anything at all. She peered into the dark and shook her head. There was no road. No road, and therefore, no headlights. She had thought—

"Amelia!"

Luke's scream cut through her thoughts. Sighing, she turned around, looking back the way she had come. She had stepped just beyond the reach of the car's high beams, but she could see him; he was standing by the driver's-side door, shifting uncertainly from one foot to the other and looking in all directions with narrowed eyes.

She stepped back into the light.

She would not speak; she folded her arms, letting her chin lift slightly, staring back at him.

"Come on," he called to her. "Let's talk about this!"

Ever so slightly, almost imperceptibly, she shook her head. Only once.

He stared back at her.

"FINE!" he roared, suddenly, and retreated to the back of the car. She could see him rummaging in the trunk—was he going to go for broke, strew her belongings into the road?

Let him. She didn't care.

Standing beside the car, he saw that she hadn't moved— was simply standing there, appraising him, *looking down on him* as she refused to come back and just talk, for crying out loud. He'd said he was sorry, hadn't he? And she was going to—what? Walk away into the dark? Walk away without her bags, her purse, walk away from *him* without so much as a conversation?

His head filled with the image of her, stumbling around in the night, lost and alone and wishing that he would come back. The night was so dark, out here—she didn't know where she was, or where she was going. She'd be frightened. Helpless.

Another minute, he thought, and she would hear the night sounds around her, hear the ominous rustling of something big in the roadside brush, and then she would come back.

He watched her.

He waited.

She hadn't moved.

He peered over the door, looked at the dashboard clock. Two minutes, tops. His eyes drifted over the interior of the car, the comfortable seats, the climate controls, the plush accoutrements of wealth. He willed himself not to stare out at her, to let her think he was going to leave, let her sweat out there in the dark and think about how stupid she'd been. His gaze settled on the passenger seat, and he started to laugh.

She had left the cigarette case. All her cash, her cards, her driver's license—they were all inside, and she wouldn't get far without them. Chuckling, he grabbed it and stepped back out of the car, brandishing it overhead and shouting at her.

"Looks like you forgot something! C'mon, Ame, come back, all right? Just—"

He stopped. She was walking back toward him, coming back, getting closer. But in the beam of the headlights, he could see that something was happening to her face. Her mouth seemed to be stretching, and then her hand was in the air, and she was smiling, and her slender wrist turned in slow motion and he stopped laughing.

She was giving him the finger.

She lowered her hand, the same queer smile still playing on her lips. He felt his ears burning, his heart pounding, his stomach beginning to churn with the realization that she wasn't coming back. She looked at him again, that same, appraising look. In the yawning dark, there seemed to be nothing but her, and the light from the car, and the car itself, and him. They were alone on a plateau of black. There was nothing but this one, bleakly lit stretch of road—but she was ready to walk out into the dark.

She was going to leave him behind. And then, for the last time, she looked back at him.

And waved good-bye.

CHAPTER 24

*I*t *was you.*

He reached for me, his mouth open, his voice saying my name. I jerked away. I was still clutching the cigarette case and driver's license—her driver's license, *hers*, stamped with the face that had stared out at me for months from bulletin boards, drive-through windows, the television screen as it played the evening news. As I fumbled with the catch on my seat belt, my panicked mind slowed just long enough to note that I finally knew the dead girl's name.

Not the dead girl.

Amelia.

Amelia Anne Richardson, age twenty-two, from a town I'd never heard of in a state I'd never been to.

James was trying to hold me, his bony fingers grasping and gripping at my arms, my sleeves, my face, trying to keep me from running. I lashed out with the hand that held the cigarette case and caught him on the ear, felt the blow ringing down my forearm as his hands flew up in surprise. The seat belt gave way with a click, snapping back with the sing of nylon, and I grabbed frantically at the door handle, and then I was outside. Running. Feet pounding, falling over the uneven ground, falling once and then again while the wind howled and tried to push me back. I cried out in frustration, plunged my hands into the dirt, propelled myself forward. I ran as lightning flashed again overhead, ran as the thunder cracked so loudly that I felt like I was trapped inside a room full of noise, ran as I heard James coming, fast, behind me.

He was still calling my name.

My feet tangled in the whipping grass and I went down again, seeing the glare of the headlights behind me, feeling the tiny zing of small cuts on my bare shins. The rain-starved weeds had turned sharp. They sliced and hissed in the wind, bending angrily toward my face, my neck, the exposed skin on my chest and back.

When I looked up, he was there.

I had forgotten how quick he was, how fast those long, coltish legs could move. I had been a fool to think I could outrun him. In this place, where there was only nothingness for miles, fields and farmland and thick woods, I had nowhere to go. And there was nobody here to help me.

I looked desperately toward the road, hoping for headlights or the sound of a motor. Seeing only darkness, black and empty, the only movement coming from the frantic tossing of the trees.

James shouted again, his voice high and tense, raised angrily over the wind. I struggled to my feet again and he moved toward me.

"Becca, stop running!"

I took one tentative step, then turned back. I stared into his face. He was lit by the headlights, his face bathed in the harsh electric brightness of the high beams, with dark shadows pooling under his eyes and in the hollows of his cheeks.

He was skeletal.

Monstrous.

This was the boy I'd thought I loved, he was chasing me down, advancing on me now with his face contorted in rage and his fist closed tight and heavy with anger.

I looked into his face and screamed.

My voice was a banshee shriek, high and raw, a sound like shattering glass and squealing tires and fingernails being dragged over slate. Full of anguish and anger. I screamed into the night, while the world howled back around me.

"What did you do, James?"

He stopped moving, his hand still hanging heavily at his side. He stared at me and shook his head, barely, and the light glinted twice in the black pools of his eyes.

"What did you do?" I screamed again. A ragged sob escaped from my lips and I swallowed hard, fighting the urge to break down. There was nowhere to go. Nowhere to go. I was here, with him. Alone, and too slow to outrun him, and too stupid to see his silences and strange anger and absence for what they were, and he was coming closer now, the wind blowing his hair back and his eyes still fixed on my face.

"Becca," he said, and his voice was like ice as the wind carried it toward me. "Becca, it's not—"

"It's her!" I yelled. "That's her, James! She's dead, she was fucking *murdered*, and you've been hiding her driver's license in your car for . . ." I trailed off, realizing how close I'd been to learning the truth, remembering how he had slapped my hand away when I reached for the glove box so many weeks before.

He took another step toward me, and I backed away. "Stay away from me!"

"Becca, just—"

"What did you do? Answer me, goddammit!" I took another step back. He moved forward. I started to sob, no longer able to hold it back, no longer sure there was any reason to. "Oh God, James, what did you do? Did you hurt her? Did you?!"

He stopped, and his eyes narrowed. His hand tensed, his fist closing tighter, the muscles in his forearm jumping and ready to move.

"Tell me!" I screamed again. I took a deep breath, clenching my hands into fists, feeling my pulse pounding in my palms like something small and terrified.

"Did you kill her?"

He didn't answer, only looked at me, working his jaw while the headlights glared against his cheekbones, his earlobes, the angular jut of his shoulders, and the long lines of his arms and legs. Inside the beam of light, small movements began to appear. A few at first, and then more, thin lines that passed through and fell to the ground with a tiny, soft sound. The field was full of it—the pattering of water, growing stronger, falling in sheets now on the leaves and brush and blades of grass. I felt cold needles on my skin, saw dark marks appearing on the fabric of my shirt as the rain came down.

Poured down.

My hair stuck in soaking tendrils to my face, and the earth below me began to soften, and still James only stood there. Silent. Unmoving. He stood there and stared, until I thought that I should run again—that I had to try—and I turned one foot to find purchase in the muddying ground, and then it came.

A whisper above the sound of the rain.

"Yes," he said. "I killed her."

AMELIA

Her hand was still in the air. Still waving as he shifted uncertainly on his feet. She lowered it only when he had slammed the door, and then, for what seemed like ages, she simply stood there.

The breeze had begun to blow again, warm and pungent with the scent of growing things. It seemed to be caressing her body as he watched, lifting her hair from her shoulders, burnishing the alabaster smoothness of her skin, pressing her thin cotton dress against the curves of her hips and breasts.

Beside the car, Luke stared wordlessly back. She was beautiful.

She was gone.

Inside his head, a blank, white, cold wall of nothingness.

She was gone.

She stared defiantly into the glare of the headlights, unable to see more than the black outline of his body, but knowing he could see her. Wanting him to see. Her chin lifted higher and she stretched herself to her full height, feeling her spine lengthen, feeling life awakening inside and all around her. The stars looked warmer, somehow, glittering and burning madly in the blue-black expanse of the sky, and the singing of insects in the trees sounded like cheering.

She thought briefly of her bag, still in the trunk of the car, packed by a girl who had better things in store for her. She stifled a laugh as she thought of her things—the book she'd planned to read on the beach; her pajamas, her jeans, her underwear, and her sensible-not-sexy bikini; even her phone, still tucked in the pocket of her abandoned purse— arriving at the beach without their owner.

He could keep them.

A smile still playing on her lips, her head held high, she looked once more at what she was leaving behind.

The cricket song reached a crescendo, urging her on and away.

She turned and began to walk.

Beside the car, Luke gripped the door with white-knuckled intensity.

She was gone.

The cigarette case hit the ground behind her with a metallic thud. She turned, seeing its contents spill and scatter, shrugging and kneeling to gather them.

She didn't see him coming.

It was over in seconds, in the flutter of an eyelid. The

widening of her eyes as she felt his shadow on top of her, the tiny, too-late movement of her hands and hips and feet as her reflexes tried to propel her out of harm's way.

And then he was upon her.

The guttural sounds of his rage, of sculpted metal against skin and bone, drowned out the indifferent song of the insects, covering the sickening crunch of her body as it crumpled and broke. Her head smacked hard against the ground, the sound ringing with horrible resonance in the empty night.

The tire iron punched against her flesh.

Brittle bones shattered.

She was crawling now, her eyes open wide in surprise, one leg dragging useless behind her. Slim arms and fingers scrabbled in the dirt. There was a flash of blond hair, a smear of red. She coughed, and one of her teeth skittered into the road. She collapsed against the asphalt.

Her hand clutched at the air, reached out toward the mountains that she could sense but not see, and then dropped.

Luke's hand, with its heavy passenger, lay still against his side.

She was gone.

The crickets were still singing.

Breathing hard, he stared down at her. His mind felt empty, wiped clean. He looked back, seeing the road lit by the glow of the headlights, seeing nothing at all but the incredible expanse of black, the wonderful smoothness of the asphalt, the indifferent yellow lines that stretched back, back, into the dark. He listened for a sound—anything, a ragged breath, a cry for help.

There were only the crickets.

He stared at the hand in the road, willing himself not to blink, not allowing himself to think of what might happen if those still, silent fingers suddenly twitched. If the night were suddenly filled with the anguished sound of a woman, screaming in pain.

Neither came.

The hand lay still.

And then, there *was* a sound.

Not her, not from behind, but out there.

Out in the dark.

It was a light scuff, the snap of a branch out in the brush, and Luke snapped to attention and ran toward the light and purr of the waiting car. Terror ran through him, diving into his veins and freezing his hands as they scrabbled at the door. *Someone was out there.*

Panicked and wild-eyed, he threw himself into the driver's seat and peered into the night.

There was another snap, and then the rustling of brush, and with a howl he pressed his foot against the accelerator, and the motor roared. There was the squeal of tires, a smell of burned rubber, and the sedan sped like a bullet. Away. Over the next rise, and the next one.

It disappeared into the night.

She was gone.

He was gone.

Out in the dark, beyond the fading glow of the taillights, beyond the reach of Luke's searching eyes, in the blackness punctured by thousands of stars, a pair of gray eyes opened and rolled blindly toward the swimming sky.

By the time James crashed out of the brush, skidding through the settling dirt and falling to his knees by the side of the road, Amelia Anne Richardson knew that she was going to die.

As graduation day faded and became yesterday, James bent over the body of the dead girl.

She wasn't dead, not yet.

She was stirring as he reached her, as he dropped his heavy flashlight into the dirt and then felt his gorge rise when it rolled away, the beam finding and illuminating her face. Her neck. Her pale arms and legs. Her body was a broken tangle of limbs and torso, splayed at unnatural angles in the soft roadside dirt, still and unmoving except for the small fluttering of fingertips, eyelashes, the pulse that beat erratically in her hollow throat. There was blood in her mouth. One of her feet began to twitch lightly against the road, tapping as though keeping time. She was wearing sneakers; the rubber instep made a dry, matter-of-fact noise as it touched down once, twice, three, and four times. Beside her, lying flat and smooth on the asphalt, was the silver cigarette case. He reached for it; his fingers left oily marks on its filigreed surface, and he recoiled and released it into the dirt.

A low cry rose in his throat as he moved over her,

looking for a place to put his hands, searching desperately for anything that wasn't too broken to touch. His hand found the curve of her shoulder, pulled gently to free her arm from where it was pinned beneath her, and as he leaned over her, a small gasp rose up from the ground below.

His skin broke into gooseflesh, and he looked down.

Her eyes were open.

She was watching him.

He bent close to her ear.

"Can you hear me?" he said.

Her lips parted; her eyes blinked. One had become glassy, unseeing, with dark spots creeping into the white from the outside edge; the other focused on him. Her dilated pupil was an endless pool of black.

She made a sound, like the slow hiss of a lazy snake, like air escaping slowly from a balloon. The blood smeared and bubbled on her teeth. One drop found its way to the twitching corner of her mouth, slipped out soundlessly, began to roll like a tiny red tributary toward the confident curve of her chin.

He felt terror slipping like a mask over his face, his eyes growing wider, his breath coming faster. The girl's eye, the one that could still see, widened in response. Her foot stopped tapping; her fingers curled themselves into loose fists. She seemed to struggle, and her lips began moving again. James panicked and pressed his hand against them. It came away smeared with crimson. He fumbled in his pocket for a kerchief, found it, dabbed it at the space between her lips.

"No, please, don't—don't try to talk. Wait—" He flung himself away from her, standing tall in the road and searching frantically in one direction, then the other, for moving headlights. For moving anything. For anyone.

"Shit!" he cried, looking back at her. The tapping foot had started its rhythmic timekeeping again. Counting down to dying, as though she meant to remind him that time was running out. "Shit, my phone, I don't have—and my car is—*hello?* IS ANYONE OUT THERE?!"

The crickets and katydids sang back in response, mocking him with echoed repeats of his own words.

Anyone? Anyone. Anyone? Anyone.

He dropped to his knees beside her again, picking up her hand—Oh, God, it was cold, her hands weren't supposed to be cold—and looked into her face. She was struggling, her lips moving, her eyes rolling wildly in her head as tears filled them and then spilled from the corners, her hands and feet fluttering like tiny birds that meant to free themselves and fly away into the night. *Let us go. We don't want to die here.*

"Listen," James said, gripping her hand tighter and staring hopelessly at a tiny muscle twitching near her hairline. She was running out of time. "I have to get my car, okay? I have to go and—" On the word, *go*, her fingers turned viselike. Her eyes rolled again and her mouth moved into a tight O shape. *No.* She dug her nails into his hand, breaking the skin, cutting tiny half-moon wounds into the roughly lined palm.

"It'll be okay," he cried, trying to pry her fingers away. "I just—I'll come back and I'll find some way to—"

The hand gripped tighter. Her good eye fixed brightly on him, opening wide and white like a beacon in the dark, and he realized with horror that the other side of her face had gone slack.

She made the hissing sound again.

And again.

Her lips pressed together and he saw her tongue moving behind them, barely moving, flicking upwards. The hissing came a third time.

He leaned closer, put his ear to her lips, heard the sound once more.

The familiar sound.

The memory enveloped him.

He was back in the sunny upstairs of the house, his house. Their house. Back in the bedroom with the yellow walls, sitting uncomfortably in a too-small chair, his fingers gently resting in the palm of a hand that looked like it was made of twigs and old leather. Her breathing was coming raggedly, now, ripping like sandpaper along the pretty, buttercup-colored paint and scraping with agonizing slowness against the floor. He hung his head and fought back tears, bit down hard on his lip to catch the strangled sound before it made its way out of his throat. He did not want to wake her.

When he looked up again, she was looking at him.

Her eyes were looking at him. She had become a series of parts, now—not his mother, not even a person, but parts. Liquid eyes and dry lips and jutting sternum that seemed ready to cut through the papery skin of her chest. The IV line snaked from her wrist to the polished silver of its stand, looming over her like a metal skeleton. The bottles of pills that lay on every surface of the room seemed like pieces of her.

He looked back at her.

Her mouth was moving.

He leaned forward, to hear—to make out whatever word was coming laboriously up through the wasted tangle of her vocal cords, pushing out through the dry cavern of her mouth.

And then he heard her voice.

He turned his face away. And let the tears fall.

"Mom, no."

Please.

"I can't."

Please.

"I *can't*," he sobbed, and began beating his balled-up fists against his knees in anguish. "Don't ask me to do that! Don't ask me again, Mom! *I can't do that!*"

When he looked up again, her eyes had closed.

Three days later, as afternoon turned to evening, the sandpaper sound of her breath slowed. And stopped.

Now, in the dark on the side of the road, James looked down as the girl's breath bubbled red inside her mouth, and her lips moved again.

Her eye had stopped rolling; it was fixed on him, on his face.

Please.

He shook his head.

Please.

And then, as the katydids sang in the trees and the stars glittered indifferently overhead, he squeezed her hand tight and bent his head to her chest.

And reached for the flashlight.

"Okay," he whispered.

Her lips stopped moving.

She blinked once, deliberately. Slowly.

Yes.

Haltingly, her head rolled to the side. She gasped in pain at the movement and then lay quiet again.

She let go of his hand.

She closed her eyes.

He looked down at her.

His hands raised, trembling, over his head.

He hesitated only a moment.

"Okay," he whispered.

And the flashlight came down.

CHAPTER 25

The rain blew in biting cascades, sheeting furiously against my body. My clothes had grown heavy, clinging in places and sagging in others, waterlogged and losing their shape. My hair hung in a limp rope, plastered between my shoulder blades. There was water everywhere, pooled in growing puddles under my feet, running in rivulets down my arms, gathering one drop at a time in the soft depression above my upper lip.

James, his face a broken wall of grief and guilt, wrapped his bony arms around his trembling body and simply stared at me.

"Why didn't you tell me?" I cried. My voice disappeared in the thudding, pattering, driving noise of the rain.

He shook his head. His lips parted—ready to explain, ready to answer the questions that bloomed in my mind with every passing second. I held my breath.

There was a flash of lightning, a deafening thunderclap, and a tree at the far end of the field exploded at its top in a shower of pink, electric sparks.

"We can't stay here!" he shouted, moving toward the car. His feet lifted away from the muck-turning ground, the twin depressions where he'd been standing beginning to fill with water, drowning grasses twining themselves around the legs of his pants.

I didn't move.

"Becca," he cried, turning back and extending his hands in supplication. Rain fell on his open palms.

"Becca, please! I'm not going to hurt you!"

Looking into his face—the long nose, the thin-skinned temples, the eyes I had stared into so many times—I knew it was the truth.

The field was a sodden mess now, nothing like it had been on the night when we parked here and I had slid, ready and willing, through the back window to lie in the flatbed. Nothing like it had been when James returned, less than an hour later, with the taste of my sweat in his mouth and my broken heart in his hands, and sat, smoking. Sucking on cigarettes, and scared of what might come next.

Nothing like it had been when he padded softly along its perimeter, drawn by the sound of raised voices by the roadside, and saw Amelia Anne Richardson there in the road, standing tall, lit by the headlights of a white sedan.

Furious, and proud, and alive.

The door slammed, we stared into the blackness, and for

a long time, we didn't speak. The rain drummed on the roof and the seat turned damp beneath my soaking body, and the dark, shiny glass of the windows became opaque with hot fog. James wordlessly reached across the seat, taking care not to touch me, finding the glove-box cigarettes where they had fallen at my feet and lighting one with a sigh. The air inside the truck turned cloudy.

I felt a hard edge cutting into the palm of my hand and looked down, looked into her eyes again, pressed my fingertips against the matte surface of her frozen face, and traced the name with my fingernail.

"Amelia Anne Richardson," I said. The words settled into the space between us. I thought, as my eyes began to water from the smoke, of how many times he must have said that name this summer, whispering it like an incantation over the rattle and hum of the motor, into the wind that whipped through the open window, into the quiet corners of empty rooms.

James looked out through the windshield, where the headlights blazed against a wall of moving water and disappeared dimly into the storm.

"Ashtabula, Ohio," he said. I looked down again, reading the unfamiliar address.

"I don't know where that is."

"It's nine hours from here," he said. He looked at me now, and his lips curled in a smile that was full of sick, sad pain. "Nine hours, exactly."

I searched his face, not understanding, then realizing as

my gaze drifted over the dull illumination of the dashboard just how many miles had appeared on the odometer in two short months.

His eyes followed mine.

"Your mom's things," I said, almost to myself. "You said you were helping—"

"I know," he said.

"How many times did you go?"

"I don't know," he said.

He had left early in the morning, always as the sun came up, always claiming excuses that would be met without question. Me, he fed the story about his mother's things, knowing that I would never doubt him, disappearing down the interstate in pursuit of answers while I sat alone and pitied his loss. He would arrive late in the day, winding through the downtown of a small city that wasn't so different than this, where people looked curiously at his out-of-state license plates and wondered who he was, this haunted-looking young man who crawled the streets in a beater pickup and stared mournfully from the window at each turn. This sad-eyed, skinny boy who drove slowly, so slowly, peering uncertainly into the waning light in search of an address. The one who parked each time, across from the same house, and watched the man who lived there as he left for work, came home, spent the evening watching sports or mowing his lawn. The one whose face grew pinched with each passing hour, until he would roar away amid the rattle of old steel and the scent of exhaust.

Disappointed.

Devastated.

Wondering how, after so many weeks, this man had not begun to wonder where his daughter was.

"That rag in your glove compartement—" I began.

He nodded, sharply.

"But . . . I thought . . . they said—" I began, then stopped. I couldn't think about Craig, couldn't let my mind open to the horror of his bloodied face, his broken nose and teeth, the sound of boots as they punched against his skin.

"No," he said, and for a moment he clenched his teeth so tightly—with so much anguish—that tremors ran the long length of his neck. "After it happened . . . I wasn't thinking. I was so scared, I was so scared that someone would come down the road and see me there, with her."

"You could have called the police—"

"And told them what?" he cried. "That she was like that when I got there? That I was just trying to do the right thing? Who would have ever believed that? Christ, Becca, not even you would have believed it."

He stopped, shaking his head. I swallowed hard but kept quiet.

He was right.

The rain was beginning to drum more lightly now, tapping its impatient fingers against the truck, as though it wanted answers too. I waited.

"I killed her," he said, finally. "That was all I could think about, that I killed her. I panicked, and I had blood on my hands, and I just grabbed everything that I'd touched—I grabbed that"—he pointed to the cigarette case—"and I bolted."

He looked into the dark.

"This is my fault," he whispered. "I did this. And now Craig . . ."

"Please don't talk about it," I said.

"How bad was he?"

I couldn't meet his eyes. When I spoke, it was to my own knees.

"Bad."

I stared again into the eyes of the dead girl. She had a pretty face, open and matter-of-fact, more friendly than the cold gray lines of the police sketch had made it out to be. She looked out at the world from the tiny square photo of her driver's license, smiling slightly, her expression full of amused resignation at having the picture taken.

Get it over with, she seemed to be saying, *and let's go.*

Wherever she was going, she had never arrived. She had been derailed, delayed, detained forever at the side of the road in a town surrounded by nothingness. The summer people would pack their things, shutter their houses, disappear for the winter and forget this place until the snow melted; the graduating classes would kiss their parents good-bye and only come home for holidays; workers at the steel plant would change shifts and crawl home in the dull twilight, only to wake up still exhausted in the cold, gray dawn. But she, Amelia Anne Richardson, would always be here.

Let's go, I thought again, and remembered the boxes that lay untouched in my bedroom, their cardboard mouths yawning with annoyance at so many weeks of emptiness. I had almost believed that they would stay that way. That I would stay this way. That there was something here for me and that this was where I belonged.

I tried again to see my future, any future. I closed my eyes. I took a breath, and the air in the car was suddenly so thick and dense that I thought I would choke.

One girl lost forever to this stagnant place was enough.

"Becca," James said. I looked up, saw him looking at me with eyes full of hope, looking at me as though he wanted to take my hand. I saw his fingers twitch, then lie still again. I stared at him in disbelief.

"I should have told you," he sighed.

"Why didn't you? All this time . . ."

He shook his head. "I thought they'd figure it out on their own, with DNA, or fingerprints, or . . . or anything. I thought someone would report her missing. I thought they'd come looking for her. And then . . . and then nobody did. And I didn't even know where to start, how to tell you, when you were just starting to trust me again."

The drumming of rain on the roof faded to a light hum. Overhead and to the west, I could see patches of star-glittering sky between the low, oppressive hang of the clouds.

James looked at me, and this time, he did reach for me.

I let him cover my hands with his, let him twine his fingers into the curl of my palm. I was still holding the cigarette case.

"I thought they would put me in prison," he said. "For . . . for what I did. Or for hiding this." He swallowed; his Adam's apple bobbed awkwardly on his neck. "And I couldn't—not then, not after the way things were between us. Not when things were so fucked up. I needed time, just enough to make things right."

I remembered his face, his voice, whispering to me in the hot, heavy air.

We can still have this summer.

"Yes," he said, and I realized that I had said it out loud.

I cracked my window, opening a sliver of night in the fogged glass. Cool air kissed my forehead. Outside, the night was thick with the smell of wet earth.

James let go of my hand, and I didn't reach for it again. I folded my fingers over the cigarette case, over the dead girl's easy smile, and clasped them tight. He looked at me, longingly, with tears beginning to rise at the rims of his exhausted eyes.

I sighed, and breathed again, and the sweet chill of rain slipped into my throat and into my belly. I opened the window wider, and the air in the car began to move, and I felt more cold on the bare, brown curve of my shoulders and along the bony length of my spine. It felt like September.

My eyes were dry as I turned to him, seeing his face lit by the glow of the dashboard light, hearing the heavy chafe of wet upholstery as I moved closer. My hand moved lightly over his shoulder, the hard curve of his collarbone, and came to rest on the flat, damp cotton that lay over his heart.

"James," I said. "Summer is over now."

There were halos around the lights that lined the parking lot as we rolled in, fuzzy spheres that hung mutedly in the damp air, glowing above empty pavement that smelled like ozone and hot tar. Beyond the window made of plate glass and steel, there was a room—green tiled, paper piled high on desks, chairs pushed askew as though people had left in a hurry. At one desk sat a young man with blond hair and tired eyes. He looked up at the sound of the car door.

"I can come with you," I said, not for the first time.

James looked at me across the hood. Steam rose between us. He sighed and shook his head, *no*, as I'd known he would. It was decided. I would take the truck; I would go home, face my parents.

He would stay.

He would go inside, and face whatever came next.

Let's go.

I stepped into the headlights. The heat from the grille was hot breath on my bare calves. His arms wrapped me like wire, all taut sinew and hard bone. I pressed my face against his shirt and inhaled, expecting the familiar, expecting to taste sweat and shaving cream and the bitter must of old smoke, but the rain had washed it all away.

I smelled only earth, dark and rich and damp.

"I'll call you," he said. He looked over his shoulder, at

the curious face of Jack Francis, at the fluorescent-lit walls and chipped tile of the station. "If I can."

"I hear they give you one phone call," I said, and he smiled, and so did I.

The wind blew through the open windows as I slipped into the driver's seat, pulling it forward, throwing the truck into gear. He stepped back, lighting a cigarette, and lifted his hand as I pulled away and into the road. Ahead of me, the asphalt stretched away, shining wetly in the glow of the headlights. Behind me, the police station was a pocket of light in the yawning dark.

I looked back, then, and saw him.

James was still in the parking lot. Watching. Waiting. A silhouette beneath the lights, smoking and tapping his knuckles against the concrete rough of the station wall. The cherry glowed, illuminating his mouth. His teeth were slick pearls behind the filter.

Watching.

Waiting.

The sick green numbers of the digital clock ticked off the minutes until dawn.

Let's go.

I didn't look back again.

EPILOGUE

On the August evening that Amelia Anne Richardson's ashes were scattered, tossed away on a gentle wind that blew coolly up the interstate and toward the coast and finally poured into the churning mouth of the Boston Harbor, a team of fast-moving police officers stormed the sides of a small, clapboard house nestled in the Cape Cod dunes. They slipped through the door in a rush of gleaming guns and starched, clean blues.

They found him sitting at the kitchen table, with his head in his hands and two months of sparse-straggle beard brushing against the yellowed collar of his undershirt.

Unwashed and whipped.

Exhausted.

He did not struggle.

As he crossed the gravel drive with his steel-clasped

hands behind, the angry ocean wind blew harder. It kicked up sand and grit, rattled the windowpanes, sent stinging granules against the sagging skin of his face and into the wet, dull glass of his tired eyes. It had been weeks since he slept.

When an officer pulled her bag from the trunk of his car, untouched and holding all the clothes she'd never worn that summer, he began to cry.

That morning, I padded softly down a worn burgundy carpet lined on each side by long wooden pews while whispers filled the space behind me. Rumors fell lightly at my heels and sank into the threadbare beige patches where too many feet had walked before.

I kept my head down.

I laid a white rose on the coffin.

I stopped in front of Richard Mitchell, whose skin and hair still glowed with the kiss of western sun, and told him I was sorry.

He turned his face away.

When I found my way outside, stumbling in my too-pointy shoes and lurching into the fresh, light heat of the morning, I discovered that the thorned stem had left an angry welt on the pale-veined swell of my wrist.

I wouldn't have forgiven me, either.

Autumn came to town before I left. It arrived unexpectedly in the old maple by the creek, where I sat with James and then sat alone, where I watched silently as reds and oranges and browns began to seep in from the corners of the leaves and the sun sank sooner, lower, vanishing with a whisper of the coming cold. The light grew slanted as the earth leaned away toward winter. In the moving air, the long green necks and slender blooms of the last late-summer hostas breathed clean white perfume into the air.

Later, after the medical examiner quietly confirmed the inevitability of Amelia Anne Richardson's death from her initial injuries—that a blow to the head had only hastened by an hour the moment when her life slipped away—he came back. We sat together in the dark, passing the bottle between us, until he pitched it away and the night was filled with the shrill sound of breaking glass, and there was nothing more to say. He would receive probation and community service for interfering with an investigation. I would testify at the trial of the men from Silver Lake, pointing at each of them in turn while terms like "internal bleeding" and "manslaughter" and "burden of proof" were tossed around the room and the piggy eyes of Craig Mitchell, martyr, gazed implacably from an oversized photograph propped on an easel.

Later, the slender hands of the boy I'd loved clasped my waist and found their way around my neck, wound into my hair, cupped the hard angle of my jaw. He tried to kiss me. I turned my face away.

"Nobody blames you," he said.

"Maybe somebody should," I said.

They called me a "cooperating witness." It's a nicer word than "guilty."

———•———

I don't come back anymore. I am gone, moved along, vanished from the minds of my neighbors if not from their memories. I disappeared down the road with the windblown ashes of a girl who died too soon. When people talk about the murder—either murder, any murder—they rarely mention my name. My parents have moved away. In the quiet streets, along the dust-dry country roads, by the brimming, babbling waters of Silver Lake, there is nothing left of us. Of me. I don't come back anymore.

But one day, some day, I will. Maybe. Hopefully. I have learned that knowing where you're going means remembering where you've been. I'm not afraid of what lurks behind me, or ahead. And while I make no promises, I have learned again, though tentatively, to make plans.

And if fate carries me back to this familiar place, I will come gladly and with hope. Tires singing on the weathered asphalt, wind whipping in my hair. I hope to search for the overgrown opening between the trees where a rutted road leads to an open field, and smell the scent of crushed grass in the fading light. I hope to always know the back roads, and the shortcuts, and the place by the side of Route 128 where the dust and dirt once mixed with blood. I hope to roll slowly past the long drive at sunset, under the high canopy of trees that reach up, away, farther and fuller with the passing years. I hope, when I pass the skeletal, half-hidden house, that he doesn't live there anymore.

That the windows are empty, and the dust has settled.

That there is nobody left to remember that summer.

That Amelia Anne Richardson is dead and gone.

And that the only thing left, heavy and sweet in the violet twilight, is the scent of wild roses.

ACKNOWLEDGMENTS

This book would not have been possible without the support, guidance, and enthusiasm of the very best people. They are so wonderful, and I am so grateful.

First thanks go to Helen Kelly and Joshua Rosenfield, also known as "Mom and Dad," for giving me life, love, and the freedom to read any book that I wanted. Thanks also to Noah Rosenfield for his incredible skill at keeping me on gchat when I should have been working. (No, really, thanks.) Thanks to Brad Anderson, who is very smart and handsome, and who could not have done more for this book without actually writing it himself.

I am deeply indebted and so privileged to have worked with Julie Strauss-Gabel, who somehow saw something in the bipolar pile of Awful that was the manuscript's earliest incarnation, who graciously offered early feedback and guidance, and who has been an invaluable, patient, terror-defusing voice of experience throughout the process of bringing it to print. Thanks to her, and to everyone at Dutton for their work on behalf of *Amelia*.

Yfat Reiss-Gendel, my agent, has been a wonderful source of support, information, and publishing savvy since our very first meeting. She also knows all the best places and has fantastic shoes.

Thank you to Mardie Cohen, who is an incredible cheerleader and the best and rarest sort of friend. To Marie DeFrancesco, English teacher, whose classes I was lucky enough to land in twice and who makes most other English teachers look like passionless dweebs. To Nicky Loomis and Kathryn Williams, inspirational writer-friends whose e-mails saved my life on more than one occasion. And to Erin King, who so kindly gave her time, thought, and critical opinion to the first of my first drafts.

And, finally, the friends who need special mention for lending an ear, raising a glass, and performing various acts of hand-holding over the past few years: Maggie Cure, bestie and fellow Girl Scout reject; Jessica Bloustein, seventh-grade life saver; Rick Marshall, who needs to write his own book; Jen Bandini, whose commitment to her art inspires; and Amy Wilkinson and Emma Chastain, who are so much more than editors. You all deserve champagne.